THE HIGH HEART

THE HIGH HEART

Joseph Bathanti

A Lynx House Book
EASTERN WASHINGTON UNIVERSITY PRESS

12 11 10 09 08 07 5 4 3 2 1

Cover and interior design by A. E. Grey.

Library of Congress Cataloging-in-Publication Data

Bathanti, Joseph.
The high heart / Joseph Bathanti.
p. cm.
"A Lynx House book."
ISBN 978-1-59766-033-4 (alk. paper)
I. Title.
PS3602.A89H54 2007
813'.6—dc22

2007038490

Eastern Washington University Press
Spokane and Cheney

For Mark Berger

J

CONTENTS

THE HIGH HEART

HOD

My first day on the job, my Uncle Pat teamed me with a little, wiry bricklayer named Shotty Montesanto who had learned the brick trade at Thorn Hill Reform School. Shotty talked like a gangster, syllable by syllable, in that halting, mannered clip, so you never really knew when he was finished with his sentences. Every day, like a uniform, he wore tight jeans and a V-necked gleaming white T-shirt. He lacquered back his silver hair, and sported a sharp, manicured goatee. On his bony chest hung a tiny gold crucifix and the horn to ward off the evil eye.

Shotty wouldn't climb scaffold. Not even the first level. He wouldn't get near it. Twenty years before, laying the last few courses in a gable three stories up, the scaffold he was on had collapsed. He fractured his skull and broke both legs, one of them shattered. Six months in the hospital. Screws and pins in his leg, and a serious, dragging limp.

He blamed it on Pat who was notorious for ignoring safety to spare his wallet. All his equipment was secondhand and wired together. His laborers crossed scaffold to scaffold in mid-air with nothing but a rickety gray plank between them and the ground.

"Skinflint Mother Huncher," Shotty said. "Hasn't bought new scaffold since World War II. And he bought that used. He still has his Baptismal money. No way I'm getting up on that wobbly shit."

Sometimes he'd apologize for what he said because Pat was my uncle, but I didn't care. It wasn't like Pat and I were close. He never said two words to me, or anybody for that matter. I didn't really know him. I went to work for him because I needed a job. I had just graduated high school and had no plans. Pat's sons all went to Notre Dame. I figured maybe I'd try night school in the fall, but I was just waiting to see what would happen, and I couldn't stand the thought of a job that kept me cooped up during the day. What I really wanted was to stay home, read Marvel comic books, and wait for the aliens that Jeanne Dixon kept predicting would swoop in on the kids one day and take us all back to outer space with them. I aimed to be first in line. But I wasn't allowed to stay home. My mother informed me that I was a grown man—my father didn't seem so sure of this—eighteen years old, and that I had to work.

My older cousins had each spent a summer laboring for Pat. Carrying a hod. They talked about it like it was climbing Mount Everest, and you didn't know nothing about anything until you had served your apprenticeship. It was the manhood ritual of the family. Work a summer carrying a hod for Pat, and then we'll see what you're made of. I didn't even know what a hod was.

The dictionary gives two definitions. One: *an open box attached to a long pole in which bricks or mortar are carried on the shoulder.* Which told me nothing until I saw one racked in the hod stand that first morning on the job. You shovel the box full of mortar, then step up to the stand, half-squat under the hod, assume its weight on your shoulder, then straighten your legs and stand, grip the pole to your chest, and step away. You then walk quickly to the bricklayers, and very gently pour—you do not dump—the mud onto the mortarboard between them. To splash is the ultimate laboring faux pas. The cardinal error. It's an insult to the bricklayers, who are the artists. The laborers are expendable. This hierarchy was immediately established.

I had no trouble mixing up my first batch of mortar: a sack of aggregate, six shovels of sand, a five-gallon bucket of water, all tossed into a gasoline-powered mixer. A giant eggbeater with a throttle cord. No problem spading the hod full. But when I stepped away from the stand, the metal V of that hod digging into my trapezius, and tried to walk, I teetered like a drunk wearing a two-hundred-pound hat. Before I and the whole thing went over, I lunged back to the hod stand and slammed it back home, sending a wash of mud all over my head and shoulders. Same with the bricks. The hod took eighteen of them. I could get it on my shoulder, but I couldn't balance it. I tried a few different approaches, but simply could not manage the physics of it.

"Jesus Christ," Shotty said. "It's a good thing you're getting paid by the hour."

I ended on that first day hauling the mud in five-gallon buckets, one in each hand. I had to stop every few yards; they were so heavy. I toted bricks in brick tongs. Ten bricks apiece, but they turned my forearms to jelly. Shotty was patient. I'd catch him smiling, shaking his head. He was Pat's fastest and best bricklayer, so he worked by himself. He needed bricks and mud in a steady stream.

I worked through lunch stocking the foundation with brick. Shotty sat in the shade and watched me. He ate two baloney sandwiches, a whole pack of Archway cookies, and drank Rolling Rock beer.

"Don't you ever tell your Uncle Pat about this," he said, holding up one of the beers. "Sit down and eat your lunch before you pass out."

"Fungol Pat," I said.

He laughed and blew out the beer in his mouth. I drank two double-Rs with him. The little seven-ounce cans. The rest of the afternoon was excruciating. I was exhausted, in terrible pain, sunburned, and dizzy from the beer. I hadn't worn a hat. My hands (no gloves) and feet (tennis shoes instead of work boots) were blistered.

Late in the day, Pat cruised by in his truck to inspect the site. He didn't say a word to anybody. His arm out the window, his sneering, handsome face lit by the sun, he watched me for a while, staggering around with my buckets of mud. Then he drove off.

Shotty gave me a lift home in his beat-up gold Bonneville. The backseat was piled with clothes and brick tools. Crushed empty beer cans littered the floor. Each time we hit a pothole mortar dust rose like smoke around us. Shotty lived by himself in East Liberty, not far from my house. When he dropped me off, he asked me what size shoes I wore.

"I don't know. Nine and a half, ten."

"Look under that shit back there. I'm gonna lend you a pair of boots."

I rooted around and found a pair of size tens, coated in a cracked layer of dried mortar.

"Take them. Good work boots are the secret to long life. And grab a pair of gloves too."

"You sure?"

"I insist."

"Thanks a lot, Shotty."

"Don't mention it."

"I'll give them right back as soon as I quit."

"At the rate you're going, I'll have them back by this time tomorrow. I'll pick you up in the morning."

"You serious?"

"Six-thirty."

Then he rumbled away in a halo of dust.

My mother knew Shotty. She said he was a slicker, that his real name was Basil, and he knew blindfolded the back entrance to every beer garden in Pittsburgh. I didn't think she even knew who

I was talking about. My dad knew him because he had labored for Pat a long time ago. But he didn't commit one way or another about Shotty, just nodded and went back to the newspaper.

He didn't just read the paper; he digested it. Every inch, including the crossword puzzles. It was he, not my mother, who cut out coupons and taped articles, cartoons, and recipes to the refrigerator. He was also the one who did all the marketing and cooking. My mother never cooked. Never. But it was their arrangement and, mysterious as it was, it seemed to work. My dad was a terrific cook. He worked as a waiter at the Park Schenley, a high-dollar restaurant near Pitt in the university district.

When I got home that first day, he was already in his tux shirt and black pants. His red waistcoat dangled from the back of the chair. He carefully folded the paper and laid it on the kitchen table. Then he started tying his tie. He was the only guy I knew who could tie a bow tie—and without even looking in a mirror. The other waiters all wore fake, clip-on bow ties.

"You know Shotty," my mother barked at my dad from the living room. In a girdle and bra, she stood in front of the screen door smoking a cigarette at the ironing board and pressed her dress. Her long, straw-colored hair was teased high on top. A furrow of black roots plowed through it. The hair in her Roman nose was long and black like a man's. Beautiful, thick black eyebrows and an unusually long septum that drooped onto her upper lip. She looked like a hawk, even when she smiled. She hostessed at a club called the Suicide King that had bands, and strippers who danced in go-go cages dangling from the ceiling. The King was on the same street as the Park Schenley. They both left the house around 4:30 in the afternoon and didn't get home sometimes until 3:00. After her shift, my mother picked up my dad—he didn't drive—and they'd meet their restaurant cronies for drinks at Delaney's or The Luna, then later to Finnegan's for a meal before coming home and emptying their pockets full of rolled bills on the kitchen table.

Theirs was a schedule that suited mine perfectly. When they were gone I was home; when they were home I was gone; and our sleep cycles took care of the rest. I believed that I *loved* them. I had no other word for how I felt, except *confusion.* But I did not like being around them when they were together. By themselves, they were fine, especially my dad; but together they were brusque and unaffectionate, always hammering away at each other. They slept in the same bed and I knew they still made love. Often when they got home early in the morning, I'd hear them. But there was something else about them. They had a history of which I was unaware—I knew that—and I was afraid that any moment they would begin to tell me about it, out of sheer spite, and I didn't want to know. Like *Invasion of the Body Snatchers*: they'd reveal their true identities, and I'd find out things about myself too that I'd rather not know.

"I know," my dad said without looking up. "I said I knew him."

"You and that goddam paper."

"Why don't you put some clothes on?"

"Don't look if it bothers you."

"What about your impressionable son here?"

"He doesn't have to look either."

My dad didn't care for Pat. Something about when he had labored for him. It had been a long time ago, early in my parents' marriage, before he scored the Park Schenley job. Sometimes my mother gave him a hard time about quitting Pat. She said they'd have more than a pot to piss in if he had had what it takes to stick it out. Pat was a millionaire, she reminded my father.

"I wasn't man enough, Rita," my dad would crack.

But something deeper ran between my mother and Pat. When their paths crossed, usually at some unavoidable family function, they merely acknowledged one another with hello and good-bye. Period. Nothing more. My dad would shake hands with Pat, and go find a chair until it was time to go. Up to the point when I called Pat for the job, at my mother's suggestion, she and Pat hadn't spoken or seen each other for at least two years. All I knew, and only in that murky way in which kids find things out, was that she and Pat had been very tight, but then they fell out over something that had to do with the church and he had slapped her around. Probably the fact that she had eloped with my father, who was not only non-Italian, but Black Irish, and Protestant as well. I'd call him an atheist, but he was too indifferent to put that much thought into it.

My dad pulled a plate out of the oven: breaded pork chops, leftover mashed potatoes he had mixed with eggs and fried into fritters. Next to it he set a salad, and rolls he brought home from the restaurant.

"Eat," he commanded.

I didn't realize how tired I was until I sat down. How achy. It was tough holding the fork because my hands were so blistered. I felt a little panicky. How long could I last at this job?

"You're all blistered up, Fritz," my dad said as he sat across the table and watched me eat.

"My feet too."

"You'll feel better after you eat."

"I'm okay."

"I know you are. You're fine. That's a mean job, Fritzy. I'm proud of you."

"Quit coddling him, Travis," my mother yelled in. "He's eighteen years old. You treat him like a baby."

"I'm not coddling him, Rita. His hands and feet are all chewed up. I don't need permission from you to be concerned."

"Concerned," my mother repeated.

I made a face at my dad like *Let it drop.* He smiled at me.

"How's the food?" he asked.

I opened my mouth to say "Good" when suddenly both of my legs cramped up. Behind my thighs and in my calves. Spasms of unbearable pain.

"What?" my dad shouted. "Rita!"

I fell off my chair and rolled around the kitchen floor. My father tried to grab me. My mother dashed in, wearing a tight black dress and high white patent leather boots with platform heels.

"My God, Fritzy. What's wrong? Fritzy!" she screeched.

"My legs," I managed. "They're cramped."

My dad had hold of me, and was massaging my legs. My thigh and calf muscles twitched.

"He's all knotted up," he said. "He probably didn't drink enough water. Get him some water, Rita."

My mother knelt to me with a glass of water. "Jesus Christ," she said. "You nearly gave me a heart attack. I thought something was really wrong. All this drama over a charley horse."

"You're a doll, Rita. A living doll," my dad said.

"Kiss my ass, Travis. He'll be alright. We're going to be late."

Each time I tried to get up, my legs cramped up again. All I could do was lie there on the linoleum.

"What do you want me to do? Leave the kid on the floor?"

"It's alright, Dad."

"You're okay down there, aren't you, Fritzy?" my mother asked.

"That goddam job," said my father.

"It's not going to hurt him. Just because you couldn't handle it."

"Don't start with that all over again."

"No, no, God forbid we bring up that tender subject. Why don't you quit?" she said to me. "Just quit the job if you can't take it. You better step on it, Travis, or we'll be late. I'll be in the car."

My father lifted me—he was strong as ten men—and carried me upstairs, and laid me in bed. He sat on the side of it, in his bow tie and red waistcoat, and rubbed lanolin on my blistered hands and feet. His hair, which had receded well off his forehead, was jet black, and curly. His eyes were black too. But his skin was fair. His face was freckled. I didn't even know how old he was. Or my mother.

"I'm sorry I let you get out of here this morning without gloves and proper shoes. I should have known better."

"That's okay. Shotty lent me some boots."

"He's not a bad guy. Full of shit. But not a bad guy. You know, Fritzy, that job's a bitch. But your mother's right. I couldn't handle it."

"Yes, you could." I didn't want to hear him talk like this.

"No, I couldn't. I try not to lie to you. I couldn't handle it. It kicked my ass. I got to get going. So long." He patted me on the shoulder.

"I'll see you, Dad."

A tiny bit later, I heard my mother trotting up the stairs, then she burst into my room, sat down on my bed, lit a cigarette and stared at me.

"What's the matter, Mom?"

"Nothing. How do you feel?"

"Better."

"Listen. I don't want you to quit that job with Pat. No matter what. You hear? Do not quit."

"Okay."

"Okay." She bent and kissed me, then ran out of the room. My dad was blowing the horn.

I never made it out of bed. The next morning I woke up feeling like hell. In my thighs and shoulders especially, like I had been pounded with fists. I limped past my parents' room where they both slept on their backs like goners, a royal blue sheet up to their waists. My dad didn't have a shirt on, his chest hairless and white as Sheetrock. His mouth was wide open and he whistled at the end of each snore like a cartoon character. Loud enough to hear above the window fan. It never cooled off upstairs. My mother wore a black velvet sleep mask, and was topless. They didn't even bother closing the door.

Downstairs on the kitchen table was a lunch my dad had packed, a thermos, my gloves, and a khaki porkpie hat with a navy and maroon band around it. Sitting on the floor were Shotty's boots, all polished up, with new laces. And a note: *Drink a lot of water and wear a hat. Lots love, Dad.* I had a bowl of cereal, then went out, sat on the curb, and waited for Shotty.

This ended up being my routine. I went to bed early, I got up early, and by the end of that first week I had abandoned the buckets and brick tongs and was humping a hod. Not as fast or as well as the others, but I was getting the hang of it. Often I dumped the mud and splattered Shotty, who would call me *strunzo*, a turd, and other dirty names in Italian, his face and immaculate white T-shirt flecked with pellets of mortar.

"Temper this shit," he'd yell, sloshing water onto his board and slicing through the mud with his trowel. "It's stiff as a wedding night peter." Or "Too soupy" when it was too wet. "Like ice cream" when it was right.

He called me *manovale*. Which means laborer. Only lower, unskilled, Shotty said. A peasant. He laughed when he said it. Because I labored for Shotty, all our jobs were on the ground. But Pat's other laborers, some my age, built scaffold, then stocked them with bricks, mortarboards and tempering cans. As the houses went up storey by storey, I watched those guys, saddled with hundred-pound hods of brick and mortar, mount the series of jittery planks that led up to the top.

In the middle of my second week, Shotty rumbled us out to a new site where Pat's outfit was doing the brick and block work on a huge plan of three-storey town houses. Shotty, because he was the master, moved inside to do all the fireplace work, and I was assigned to two other bricklayers, Ernie and Ted. They had known my dad from the job. Ernie was an easygoing old guy, about to retire. He was crinkled up with arthritis and had a pair of hands that looked like trowels. Ted was a hotshot, in Shotty's league as far as craft, and he rode me pretty hard. When I dumped a load that ended up splashing them, Ernie would laugh and say, "Thanks for the bath, kid." But Ted would get pissed. He didn't like a speck on him. He'd glare at me and say, "What the fuck?" He moved like a machine, and I had trouble keeping up.

"Mud," he'd scream. "Mud, dammit. Jesus Christ. I need mud."

Toward the end of the third day, the first storey was completely bricked, and Ernie, Ted, and I started building scaffold: rusting, cast-iron bucks, shaped like football goalposts, anchored with struts and bolted together. Across the bucks, planks were laid side to side to make a platform. Which is what the bricklayers stood on as they worked. At the base of the scaffold, to level it and keep it from falling over, we scotched in pieces of brick and wood scraps. A cleated plank, like a ramp, up which the *manovale* trudged with a hod on his back, was stretched from the ground to the scaffold.

Once we had it finished, Ted told me to stock it. It wasn't a big deal to walk up the plank, nailed down at about a thirty-degree angle, with the hod of bricks, and place a few on each side of the mortarboards situated around the perimeter of the building. We were only about ten feet off the ground and the height didn't bother me at all. After it was stocked Ernie and Ted started laying brick and I hustled up and down with mud. Ted gave it to me the whole time. It was like he had this hard-on for me. Everything I did was wrong. I didn't open my mouth, though I wanted to bash his head in with my hod. Instead, I just hustled all the more. I was Pat's nephew—everybody knew this—and I didn't want anyone taking it easy on me because of it.

Shotty, his T-shirt dotted with the black mortar always used to brick fireplaces, came out every now and then to check me out. He cupped his eyes and gazed up at me maneuvering that scaffold and shook his head. He and Ted, the maestro bricklayers, didn't like each other.

Pat made a couple appearances every day to replenish the water barrels for the mixers. He'd speak to the bricklayers, but not even a grunt for me. I knew, however, that he was watching me. Not really with approval, but a grudging, almost disgust, it seemed. But I don't know. I figured it was me.

I learned to lay off the Rolling Rocks at lunch. I found a place in the shade, ate my lunch, smoked a couple cigarettes, drank coffee from my thermos, and watched beautiful women get out of beautiful cars as they cased the new town houses. I got brown and strong. Sometimes I'd catch my own eye in a storm window on the site, and not recognize myself.

At home the scene remained the same: my parents sharing the same pack of Pall Malls, same Zippo, same ashtray, my mother in her underwear with her head upside down in the sink touching up her roots, my dad scotch-taping recipes he'd scissored from the newspaper to the fridge, wrangling that black hank of material into a perfect bow at his Adam's apple. They'd both be sweating, a revolving fan on a pole ruffling the dusty sheers at the open window.

They'd sit with me if they had a few minutes and watch me wolf down whatever my father put in front of me. My mother always wanted to know if it bothered me that she didn't do the cooking. No, I'd tell her, which was the truth. That isn't what bothered me. Sometimes she'd tell me how handsome I was, what a fine man I was turning into now that I was working for Pat. Pat was stationed in Italy during World War II. My dad hadn't gone to the war. My dad was a gutless wonder, she'd say. "Gutless wonder." She used this on my dad like a pet name, and most of the time he just smiled at her and said nothing.

"You're a witch, Rita," he'd sometimes say. "A magnificent witch."

"Kiss me, gutless wonder."

And they'd kiss.

"Some day, Rita. Some day."

"Some day, what? Some day you're going to grow a set of balls? Some day you're going to hit me?"

"I don't hit women."

"Oh, why don't you go ahead and hit me, Travis."

Hit her, Dad, I'd think, losing my appetite and walking out to the alley to get away from them.

After they left, I'd sit and stare at the kitchen wallpaper, listen to the neighbors gathering on their stoops, the little kids out in the street playing Indian ball. I'd read comic books and watch TV, sometimes wander down to the school yard and sit on the steps and smoke cigarettes. Often I'd think of things I shouldn't: tanned women, no older than my own mother, really, like the ones I'd see strolling around the site in madras wraparound skirts and white sleeveless blouses. Natural blondes with gorgeous teeth and blue eyes who saw the rest of their lives stretching endlessly toward the horizon like an untroubled sea. You could still smell on them the baby oil and chlorine from the country club pool. At home they had housekeepers. On their kitchen counters were bottles of vermouth and blenders with which they made their children milk shakes every night. The sun was their friend. And money and ancestry.

Under that soft cotton, what were their bodies like? The sheets they slept in? Like lying down in a field of what I imagined a cotton crop might be like, then a gentle snow atop it? Spotless. Immaculate. Whiter than Heaven. Their lips at your ear describing love. Their hands, their beautiful, lovely hands purifying your body like the Lord God of Hosts.

That's the kind of woman Pat had married. One of those blondes who smiled all the time and meant it. A woman who came from a family of doctors and judges, bred on the aristocratic side of the Allegheny River. Who gave him children, filled with the vigor and optimism of the New Frontier, who looked like an ad for Kodak. Pat had crossed over. He knew the secret. How to step out of his red muddy pickup at six o'clock into the sanctum of cordials and dinner jackets. A deacon at Saint Paul's Cathedral, he had even stayed with the church. He played golf with the bishop. Handsome, distant Pat. Yes, he knew the secret. The secret was money. My parents knew that too, I guess. Though they were just unlucky. But there was something more than just luck.

I had never had a real girlfriend. Only those wrestling matches in Highland Park with dark girls that passed for love or whatever. That required two showers after the dirt and sweat and mosquitoes to feel clean again. I couldn't think too long about the whole thing because I'd start to cry. I was alone in the house. It would have been okay to yell and scream and beat on things. No one could distinguish my agony from anybody else's in the neighborhood. We lived that close. Row houses, party walls, alleys.

The streetlights hummed outside my bedroom window, and I'd simply turn my face to the wall. I was usually in bed by nine, worn out by the hod. I never prayed to God. I felt like a mongrel, and looked like one too. I'd think about my future, but all that appeared on the screen was static, a scrambled signal. Jesus Christ. I knew my mother was a stripper, not a hostess. And I had no idea what was up between her and my father. Then, for some reason, I'd start worrying about the scaffold, the gable I'd be climbing the next morning with a hundred ungainly pounds on my back, Ted yapping at me to step it up, goddammit, as I tightroped on a moldy two-by-six across the abyss.

I wished I could be a mutant—shit, I was a mutant—like the ones I read about in Marvel, someone with phenomenal secret powers. Like flying or clairvoyance. Or even just plain goodness. I'd settle for optimism. That seemed a secret power in itself. I craved a future as much as anyone. I craved love. Desperately. But I knew—I knew, I knew, I knew—that all there would be for me was running away. If I split—when I split—no one would ever know I had left.

In the morning, when I padded out of my room just before six, my parents would be sprawled in bed, mostly naked in their bargain, whatever the hell it was.

One day Ted called my dad a faggot. We were nearly finished with the second storey of one of the town houses. Shotty was downstairs laying firebrick with black mortar. Every once in a while you'd hear an elegant string of made-up Italian profanity, and Ted and Ernie and I would laugh. I was humping double-time to keep Ted and Ernie supplied. They were laying used brick—antique brick—so I had to chip all the old mortar off with a brick hammer before loading them in the hod. I broke as many as I cleaned. My hands were torn up. It was hot and getting ready to rain. We wanted to get done before it opened up, then raise the scaffold for the next day before we went home. Ted had been busting me all day about how slow I was. I was costing him money. I had tripped over the plumb line twice. Good thing Pat was my uncle. On and on.

I don't know if I was meant to hear it. But as I navigated along the scaffold with a hod of mud on my neck, Ted said plenty loud to Ernie, "Travis Sweeney is a faggot." His back was to me, but Ernie looked up like, "Uh-oh," when he saw me. Then Ted, who, just from the expression on Ernie's face, knew I had heard, swiveled around and smiled. Smiled at me after he had called my dad a faggot. He was on his knees. The empty mortarboard was between him and Ernie. In one of his hands was a brick and in the other his big trowel with a wet slab of mortar on it.

I stood there like a jerk for what seemed like a long time, taking in Ted's clean-shaven unapologetic smiling face. Then I dumped my hod. On him. Most of it oozed out over his head and face. He aged forty years. All that gray. A hundred pounds of age. Like he had just surfaced from a bog.

I clutched the hod. Out in front of me like a huge battle-axe. Ted jumped up and came at me with the trowel, wielding it like a switchblade, jabbing it toward my face, grabbing hold of the hod pole with his free hand and trying to wrest it from me. He cursed me, but every time he opened his mouth mud seeped into it. He dropped the trowel and with both hands grabbed onto the hod pole and pushed me toward the edge of the scaffold. I couldn't hold him back. I was going over. No doubt. If I don't land on something, I thought—a spike, an angle iron, one of the carpenter's power saws, whatever, there was lethal refuse all over the site—maybe I wouldn't get messed up too bad. We were only one buck up. I don't know how Shotty dragged his gimp self up the plank, scaffold phobia and all, but suddenly as I was getting ready to tank, he lurched up behind Ted, put the choke hold on him, and, brandishing the business end of my brick hammer, told him he was going to make *giambotta* of his face if he didn't let me go.

When I got home that night, I studied my dad: as he throttled his newspaper, spooned up the Welsh rarebit he knew I loved so much, and asked me how the job was going; confessed in that offhand way of his that he could never cut the mustard, that that job had put a first-class hurting on him, that he was proud of me; as he zipped up my mother's skimpy sharkskin dress, and ran his hands across her rump.

She told him he had the hands a safecracker and the gumption of a baton twirler. She'd make a man of him some day. He said women like her made men feel like real heroes, like Medal of Honor winners. That if we could package her particular brand of warmth, then there wouldn't be those posters of hungry stick-thin Biafran kids, there wouldn't be any need for bomb shelters and civil defense drills. She was some classy broad, he said.

"And you're some poet," she snarled, but couldn't help smiling. Then she wheeled around and bashed him with a kiss that was like a sucker punch. "My gutless wonder," she whispered, her mouth sucking the soul right out of him. He was hurting when she laid off, but he smiled and winked at me.

The next morning they swooned naked across each other in bed like felled trees, her hair gauzing his face, their sweating, smoky clothes commingled on the linoleum at the bedside. Ted had gotten to me with that *faggot* remark. It didn't mean anything. I knew that, but still, my dad had punked out on the job. I had heard him say himself he couldn't cut it. Every time I squatted under the hod I thought of him, dying under that condescending sun and the eyes of those unforgiving bricklayers. Silent Pat rooting for him to fall on his face, so he could punish his sister, my mother, for who knows what. Marrying my father, Travis Sweeney. There was more. There was always more. But again, the last thing I ever wanted was for their little lockbox of secrets to be pried open.

For the rest of the week, Ted didn't clearly speak to me. The only words out of his mouth in my direction were "bricks" and "mud." Pat showed up on Friday to lay block in an adjacent foundation, something he did only if he was short-handed. He was sure to have heard what happened with Ted and me, but of course he'd never let on. We were working the third storey, moving up to brick my first gable. From my perch on a two-by-twelve, I glanced down at him. In one hand he held a termite, an immense heavy block used in foundations. He wore a sky blue cap and a white football jersey. He moved with speed and parsimony, his trowel knifing in and out of the mud and icing those leaden termites that he manhandled into somebody's future like they were nothing. I didn't really like him. I couldn't. But he was beautiful. If you could say such a thing. He looked up at me, thirty-five feet above him, in midair with a full hod of bricks, and paused. Then raised his trowel, and smiled, ruefully, derisively. Just for a second, then went back to work. I don't know. I didn't take it for any kind of benediction. Nevertheless it equaled something, and for that second I felt pretty good, like maybe I belonged there.

I was between the third tier of scaffold and what we called a foot-hop where Ted was working by himself. The scaffold shook a little. Which wasn't uncommon once we were that far off the ground. I took another couple of steps. The plank shimmied. And I don't know. I froze. I panicked. Ted screamed, "Bricks." He wanted bricks, goddammit. He wanted bricks. I took a step toward him and then I lost my balance, the hod pulling me one way and then another.

When I looked down, I could tell it was late in the day. The masons and carpenters and electricians were loitering below, cleaning and stowing their tools, lighting cigarettes, empty mortar bags and shingles blowing about their work boots. Ramparts, smoke and dust, gleaming lethal steel. Already a few pickups, red dust hanging over them, wound their way out of the site along the hacked-out dirt road. It was the time of day I had come to love, when everyone lays down his tools and begins to ponder how many minutes he has on earth until bedtime. The in-between blessed part when you're about done weltering it out, but you're not back in that other world yet. The one of wives and kids and people who work inside sitting down all day.

All of those guys. They were peering up at me. Waiting for me to fall. So they could make a story of it: *Some mongrel kid. No one even knew his name. Who froze up and fell climbing his first gable, then raced the bricks to the clay. And some well-to-do family pitched their kids' swing set where he hit, never imagining that the first green thing planted there wasn't their sod, but that green kid who never had a chance anyhow. Pat's nephew. It's a shame, but it happens. Thank God, it wasn't me.*

I had to have been scared, but what concerned me most, idiotically enough, was reclaiming my ballast and getting those bricks up to Ted. That deadweight on my back, however, had a mind of its own, and each move I made sent me swaying. I took my eyes off the ground and gazed up at Ted. He stared at me with astonishment, pity, as if I had already begun to plummet.

And then I knew I was going over. Because I had to. I couldn't cheat these glorious pigheads gathered beneath me. They loved me, the way they looked at me, but only if I died at their feet. Like a man. A scoop of clouds crossed the sun. I thought of my dad, how he was the brave one. Brave for quitting, for not caring what people would say. Balls as big as cement mixers because he didn't give a shit. I was the coward. Sheer cowardice, greed, and ignorance kept me humping for Pat because I cared, after all, what people thought of me. I had something to prove. I didn't want all those cousins of mine, the ones I'd probably never see again, the ones who had looked down on me ever since I could remember, thinking poorly of me, calling me a sissy, because I didn't have what it took to carry a hod. I was too scared not to die for all of them. Pat, my mother, my cousins, the guys waiting down there. Not my dad, though. He'd say forget about it. Come on home. He'd make me bacon and eggs. I saw the golden Allegheny, far off, lumbering into the west, sucking the sun down into it.

I looked down again and there was Shotty.

"Throw the hod down," he said loudly, but very calm.

For some reason, it didn't register. I tried to take a step toward Ted, froze again, the hod driving me over.

"Let go of the hod, Fritzy," Shotty screamed. "Now, dammit. Throw it down."

It fell from my shoulder face-first, the bricks missiling out into the earth ahead of it, scattering everyone, then crashed with a metal thud, and bounced. I collapsed to my hands and knees and edged backwards down the plank toward the scaffold.

Once I was back on the ground, Pat hurried toward me. He looked worried. I guess I had almost gotten killed. If it hadn't been for Shotty. All the guys just gaped at me. I smiled at Pat. I was relieved as hell. He grabbed me with both hands by the shirt front, spun me and got me into a headlock, then muscled me over to his truck and threw me against it.

"Get in," he said.

"What are you doing, Uncle Pat?"

"Get in the truck." He lifted his fist. I shied back. "I'll bust your empty head open. Get in the truck."

I climbed in—I heard the guys laugh as we pulled away—and sat there staring at his profile the entire time he silently sped me home. He had a day's growth, black as soot, with a long white scar along his jaw that looked like an eight-penny finishing nail. Squared-off sideburns. He didn't smoke. He didn't drink. He was a deacon in his church, president of the Holy Name Society, a revered father and husband. It occurred to me that it was Shotty who called out to me. Not Pat. Pat would have caught the bricks instead of me. He would've docked me for every busted brick, dead nephew or not. I think I loved Pat, as much as I hated him, and was even tempted to tell him this. Much as it shamed me, what I wanted most was for him to love me.

My parents were at the kitchen table playing Scrabble, their hands curled around urine-colored drinks like hand grenades. They seemed pissed at each other. My mother wore a robe and my dad was in a pair of boxers and an open pajama top. The radio was on.

Pat didn't knock. Just marched me into the house by my arm, and kind of pushed me. My mother, her robe half undone, walked into the living room, the only other room downstairs, and just stared in shock. As far as I knew Pat had never been in our house before. Then she smiled the most beautiful smile, and said, "Patrick." Down the short hall in the kitchen, my dad studied the Scrabble board. He took a sip of his drink, turned up the volume on the radio, then picked up the paper and opened it in front of his face.

"He's finished," Pat announced.

"What happened?"

"He nearly fell off a scaffold."

"Oh, my God." She looked at me, horror on her face. The paper rustled in the kitchen. Music. The tink of a bottle refilling a glass. The robe was open to her navel.

"I don't want him on the job any more. He doesn't have the spine for it."

She took a step closer to Pat and said, "Whatever you think."

Then she launched herself at him, threw her arms around his neck, and held tightly to him like a little girl, her eyes closed, her cheek nailed against his chest. She sounded like she was crying. Pat's arms levitated up, as if of their own volition, to comfort her. Instead he went for her hands clasped at the back of his head. But he couldn't get her off.

Finally, he grabbed her hair and yanked, until she peeled off, with a little cry, her robe dangling off her shoulders, exposing her. Pat raised his fist with my mother's bleached hair clutched in it and lorded it above her like he was going to pound her. Then he threw the bright yellow shock in her face. She had to spit some of it out of her mouth. It fell down onto her breasts, then to the floor.

My mother glared up at him like some savage Joan of Arc, and went for a big turquoise ashtray. I swear Pat let her hit him. Never moved. Didn't raise an arm to deflect it. The thing weighed a couple pounds, I bet, and it shattered on his head like hitting a rock. Pat didn't flinch. No blood. Nothing. He took it like some indestructible mutant villain, held his ground for a moment to let the fact of his invulnerability sink in, then walked out the door.

The other, the second definition for hod is *praise; confession.* The etymology is, I believe, Yiddish and, of course, has nothing to do with bricks and mortar. I should have told Pat that he was full of shit, that I did have the spine even though I knew I didn't. What I wanted most was my dad to set down the newspaper, come in and call him out. Beat the hell out of him. But that isn't what would have happened. Pat would have torn him apart and my dad knew it. I was glad Pat had left. He could have done a lot of damage and I sure didn't want to tangle with him. My parents, in their own weird way, knew what they were doing. They at least knew more than I did. The things I never wanted to know.

In a minute, my father called in to my mother from the kitchen that it was her turn, and she went back and they finished their Scrabble game. My dad won, as always. He knew a lot of words. Then they got up and got ready for work, with the usual bickering and one-liners, and I ate the supper my dad served me. For dessert he made me a Boston cooler: half a cantaloupe, with vanilla ice cream tamped into the crater.

THY WOMB JESUS

For indeterminate amounts of time, my mother refused to speak to my father and me. It always started with my father. Usually some trivial spark between him and my mother—what he said or didn't say, innuendo, his tone, anything really—triggered her silence. It could last half an hour, two days, two months. My father would speak to her: "Good morning, Rita." "Telephone for you, Rita." "Rita, have you seen my belt?" "Where's the aspirin? Rita, will you please tell me where the aspirin is?" Nothing. My mother was unswerving in her devotion to silence, her perfect work of art: a statue in the immense marble hall hushed by billows of ether. Face impassive, eyes vacant, she rendered all before her nonexistent.

Inevitably, her silence slabbed over me too. I could feel it coming, slowly, inexorably, like a massive weather front. Whatever lit in her hands slipped from them like mercury: a clove of garlic, keys, her cigarette lighter. She put fire to cigarette after cigarette, then forgot them. Each ashtray filled with smoking worms of ash.

I studied her as she prowled the house like a strange, sidling dog: painting her nails, tongue out, the fumes from the polish;

the net of hair spray hanging in the bathroom, the faces she made as she daubed on makeup, the bullet of red lipstick racing around her mouth.

Standing in the bathroom door, I tried to talk to her. In bra and half-slip, teasing high her mustard-colored hair as if I weren't there. About what I was doing in school. How I was tripped up in the spelling bee by the word *sapphire,* two *p*'s, not one. Maybe I'd try out for Little League. Beside the rack of pink curlers on the sink I set the cup of tea I had fixed her, and a picture I had drawn of a house. I didn't want her to point her invisible ray at me. I didn't want to disappear. She'd swipe the yellow tangles out of the rat-tail comb and drop them, the planet of dead hair floating slowly down to the wastebasket. Then she'd walk through me like I was mist.

The longer it went on, the more convinced I was that she really didn't recognize my father and me, or even see us, for that matter, that she had crossed into a shadow universe, like villains in *Superman* who languished in the fifth dimension, waiting to reenter the real world through an imperceptible seam. Gone from us forever, unreachable as a zombie. I figured it was my fault, though I was never sure what I had done.

"You didn't do a damn thing," my father assured me from his perch of apathy and wisdom. "She can't help it. It's that deranged Italian blood. It takes her over like a spell."

My mother hadn't spoken to us in two weeks. She hadn't eaten in days. We heard her in the living room, smoking one cigarette after another: a sough, then furious in-suck, the match fizzing, the crazy engine inside her carping. He shook his head and smiled like *What can you do?* Then brewed another pot of coffee, mixed a VO and water, no ice. It was time for him to start thinking about brushing the lint of his burgundy waistcoat, peeling a heavily starched tux shirt out of the dry cleaner's cellophane. He was a waiter at the Park Schenley. He needed to get moving, but he'd never rush. *Life is short, Fritzy.*

We sat at the kitchen table—red Formica and red vinyl and chrome chairs—playing two-handed poker, gambling blue-tipped wooden kitchen matches he lit the gas burners with. He patted his beloved newspaper: LBJ had just sent the first combat troops into Vietnam to protect an American air strip near Da Nang. There was a picture of two Marines in full battle gear carrying mortars. They smiled. Around their necks were garlands of flowers. Vietnamese girls with long straight black hair and plain white dresses walked behind them.

"This is the beginning," my dad predicted. "A revolution's coming."

I didn't know what he meant. He'd been to Niagara Falls and the Chicago World's Fair. His mother and father were dead. He seemed to have little past. When my mother was on a tear, I was always afraid he'd pack his bags and leave. Travis Sweeney. That was my dad. And my mother: Rita Sweeney. Rita Schiaretta. Shotgun bride and groom. My father knew how to get along in the world.

We shoved cards and matches back and forth across the table, killing time, glancing every now and then through the screen door at the kids playing Wiffle ball in the alley, sparrows swooping out of the eaves, the vaguest breeze, warm, with the scent of spearmint and wild onions, ruffling the dish towel draped over the oven handle. In the last moments of spring, before the house got so insufferably hot that the bedclothes sweated, and would mold if not changed every two days, and the clock faces bearded with condensation so we never knew the time.

But spring, what was left of it, was different. Just my father and I before he had to hit the job. He and my mother always traveled to work together. Even when they weren't speaking. Over time, they had perfected a way to make do without opening their mouths. She hostessed at a club near the Park Schenley. They had a faded 1961 two-door beige Impala. My mother did all the driving. My dad didn't even have a license. We could hear her smoking and a guy's somber stagy voice on TV. One of those afternoon shows.

My father asked me what I wanted to eat. He handled the cooking. I didn't know what I felt like, just that I didn't want him to leave. Or my mother either. It was okay, having her in the other room with the TV talking—now it was a woman in an imploring voice—almost as if she were calling to me and my father, telling us where she was. She had been lost, but now she was back. Sun slanted in through the screen door and lit up the red table face like stained glass tablets of blood. On it were an ashtray, cigarettes, and salt and pepper shakers: a black man with white hair and beard and a slouch hat, and an Aunt Jemima woman.

What my father had been telling me was that he and my mother were trying to have a baby: as he broke the eggs for the omelette, whacked in some Velveeta cheese and chipped ham, sprinkled pepper, canned mushrooms, and black olives, buttered two pieces of Italian bread and threw them in the oven to toast, sliced a tomato, shelled a grapefruit, and boiled water for my cup of tea. Talking as he worked, his back to me, shirt off. He was broad and white, his sides butting out a bit from his belt. In the middle of his back on either side sat vents of excess flesh.

On the stove top, propped against the lime-green wall, was a framed placard: *Rita is boss of this kitchen, and if you don't believe it, start something.* Beneath the script was an old crank-up telephone and a compote with scraggly yellow flowers looping out of them. Above it on the windowsill rested a planter, a ceramic Madonna and Child with a bright green vine of philodendron spraying up over the heads of mother and baby, pink cheeks, lips scarlet, eyes closed, cheek to cheek, haloes locked inseparably like twin suns. Our Lady's soft blue cloak. Thirty-three years before little Jesus would meet His mother on the execution road.

For some reason, my mother couldn't get pregnant. It was like she was trying to prove something, having another baby, my father said. He didn't entirely understand it, but he was willing to go along with it—with anything, really—if it made her happy. I loved the idea of a baby, how we'd all have to walk on tiptoe and whisper, how we'd observe its lovely fragile presence like a sacred office.

"She'll never be happy though," my father said, putting the food in front of me. Then he lit a cigarette and sat down to watch me eat.

Wearing a frazzled pink slip, my mother burst into the kitchen and plopped down at the table.

"Good afternoon, Rita," said my father.

"Hi, Mom."

"No one talk to me." She speared my father's cigarette from the ashtray and puffed on it. She glanced at us. Furtive, like just paroled, or coming out of anesthesia. All comparisons are useless. She was Rita Sweeney, Rita Schiaretta. She didn't give a shit about anything. That she had spoken, however, even to warn us not to speak to her, was a good sign.

As we looked at her, one of her hoop earrings fell off her lobe and rolled under the refrigerator. She threw herself into the giant white Amana as if to push it aside.

"Rita, I'll move the refrigerator. Calm down," said my father softly.

She grabbed the broom and pounded the refrigerator until on its blank face popped little craters, and black scars where the paint chipped. My dad just sat and watched her, mesmerized, as if the Blessed Mother had stepped off her pedestal in the sanctuary at Saints Peter and Paul, and he were witnessing it. He loved her for this very kind of thing.

When she wore out, she dropped into a chair at the table. My dad got up and shoved the fridge a few feet across the floor, retrieved the earring, and handed it to my mother.

"Thank you, Travis," she said, breathlessly, her body suddenly limp, grateful to be back in the world of words.

"It's almost time to leave, Rita."

"We can take a minute, though, can't we? To sit here and pull ourselves together."

"A minute's fine, Rita. I think we can take a minute. How about something to eat?"

"Something to eat," my mother repeated dreamily.

"You should eat something, Mom," I ventured, my first words to her in days.

She reached across the table and squeezed my hand. "You care about your mother, don't you, Fritzy?"

Such questions aren't meant to be addressed. I was sure of that fact even then, but the boldness of it startled me, and I never got around to answering. She wouldn't have heard me anyhow. She was like an amnesiac during the first few minutes of discovering her true identity, still two people. Just standing on the narrowest strip of earth, a brink on either side. My father took care not to startle her.

"I'll make you anything you'd like, Rita," my father said gently.

"Just tea, and we can pretend that I've been sick, but the worst of it is behind me, that everyone is relieved to the point of tears, and I'll lounge on the couch with a blanket and watch TV."

"We can make all that happen, Rita. But you don't have to be sick."

"I don't?"

"Of course not, but we're going to have to get a move on or we'll be late for work."

"I don't think I can go today, Travis. Please don't make me go."

"You don't have to go, Rita. We'll call in and tell them we're sick."

My father lifted my mother from the kitchen chair, carried her into the living room, and laid her on the couch while I ran upstairs for a blanket to cover her, even though the house was quite warm.

My father and I sat with her while she daintily sipped her tea.

When my mother found her voice again, after a binge of silence, it was as if she had discovered with it the secret of lovely, glowing women, the kind like June Cleaver and Donna Reed who always wore pearls and dresses even during housework, who never raised their voices, who walked in a nimbus of chastity and gentility that bathed everyone around them with light and beauty.

There my mother reposed, bed pillows wreathing her head, blanket pulled to her bodice, covering the gaudy slip, placing her palm to my father's cheek, "Travis, you are so good to me," looking with absolute wonder and candor into his eyes.

He winked at her and patted her hand. "You're doing fine," he whispered.

"I am, aren't I? Tell me I'm doing fine, Travis?" She even affected the breathless diction of those perfect women.

"You're doing fine, Rita."

She looked at me as though I were a wholly remarkable child, occasionally pulling me to her, running her hand through my hair, kissing my cheeks and forehead, then holding me a little ways from her and studying me.

"So what have you been up to, Fritzy?" she asked like she had never met me. What was my favorite subject in school? Did I like my teacher? What was her name? Was she pretty?

By then my father had called in sick for both of them, put Frank Sinatra on the dusty hi-fi, and set up the Monopoly game.

"Let me fix you something to eat, Rita," my father offered.

"Can I wait just a minute, Travis? I don't have to eat this second, do I? Not while everything is almost making sense? While you and Fritz are sitting here like soldiers at my feet?"

"Take your time, Rita. There's no rush."

"No rush," she repeated, hunkering down on the couch like a child recovering from a long illness, grateful to be alive, evangelized by each mundane fact orbiting her.

We moved our tokens round the Monopoly board. My father, the ship; I, the race car; and my mother, though I had never seen her touch needle or thread, the thimble.

The neon board filled with our industry: shiny green houses and red hotels, occupied by people moored to the earth, like us, through kindness and optimism; the dizzying speed with which we hurtled along the avenues; the hazards of confinement and decrepitude; the thrill of the crisp bills doled into my palm by my father each time I passed Go. My mother leaning down from the couch to smooth the hair along my forehead, her tired and beautiful laughter as the night birds swooped in and the house darkened feebly. It was summer coming in. I hadn't noticed how time had passed. "You're growing up," my mother said. "Isn't he, Travis?"

"He is," agreed my father.

Two sweethearts and the summer wind, sang Sinatra.

"I think I'm pregnant, Travis."

My father beamed and patted her hand. "That would be something, Rita."

"Would you like a little brother or sister, Fritzy?"

"Yes," I said, thinking again about our house suddenly rarified and mysterious, the sacristy hush, the overflowing kindness. That infant turning in its pristine sleep, breathing the same air as me. I'd never be alone again. "Yes," I said again, and my mother clutched me to her while my father continued to smile.

"I'm so hungry," my mother exclaimed.

"Coming up," said my dad, getting to his feet.

"I have this awful craving."

"Name it."

"You'll think I'm awful."

"Rita."

"I'm dying for canned ravioli. Chef Boyardee. That's awful, isn't it?"

"It's not awful, Rita."

"I must be pregnant. What else could it be to have me craving canned ravioli, of all things. But it sounds so good."

My dad whipped out a five and handed it to me. "Fritzy, run up to Chookie's and buy a can of raviolis."

"Two cans, please. I'm starved."

"Two cans, and keep the change," my father added.

I ran to the store in the fading light. On Chookie's corner loafed the hoods, pitching craps for smokes, sweating in their motorcycle jackets and greasy boots, cruel swirling glistening hairdos and sneers that scared me, though they never said a word. Like me, they were in-between, inconsequential, innocent really. Another season and they'd stink of reefer and wouldn't be able to afford their leather coats—not even in the proper season, having sold them and everything else for junk. By then there would be prison bars on Chookie's windows. A revolution was coming.

Inside I paid for the ravioli, then, drinking an Orange Crush, strolled home slowly, dreaming about the baby, in the last of the light. It was a script I could never have imagined. At the point of disaster and disgrace—my mother never opening her mouth to my father and me again, our family dissolving like salt in water—there had come the reversal, that moment of catharsis: something as unexpected, but absolutely inevitable, as a baby. Nothing, after all, was wrong at my house. My mother and father loved each other. They loved me. Soon I'd be a big brother, no longer the only child. Well-being overflowed the streets. I felt it in the beatific glow of the Collins Avenue streetlights. I had even seen it in the faces of the hoods. We had all felt it. It had been there all along like the Kingdom of God. Had it been *Leave It to Beaver* or *Father Knows Best*, the episode would have ended right there with the theme song, my scuffed All Stars slapping me home across the glittering concrete, the moral scrolled across my gleaming face like scripture.

But I was compelled by fate to keep walking toward our little half-brick rental where my parents and the new baby awaited me. Night had fallen. The house was dark. I switched on a lamp. On the floor the Monopoly board had been ransacked: the shimmering green houses and bright red hotels toppled, money and deeds scattered, my mother's pink slip discarded along baby blue

Oriental Avenue, a door or so down from the jailhouse. My mother and father were gone. As if blown away by the summer wind. Then I heard them upstairs. I wanted to run up and tell them I had the ravioli, but I knew all about what was going on. I set the cans on an end table. And turned on the TV to smother the noise they were making.

When they came down a few minutes later, they were smiling. My mother wore a chartreuse bathrobe knotted loosely at her waist and smoked a cigarette. She had put on red lipstick and brushed her dandelion hair. My dad was still shirtless, but red-faced and mottled across his chest.

"I got the raviolis," I proclaimed.

"Why don't we have a little drink here?" my mother said. She swept by me into the kitchen and took a seat at the table. My father and I followed her. "Make us a drink, Travis," she ordered.

"What do you want, Rita?"

"I don't know. How about something to make a girl think twice about . . ."

"About what?" my father asked.

"I don't know about what. Just something to make a girl think twice."

My father bent under the sink, and yanked out fifths of Seagram's VO, Old Granddad bourbon with the seal unbroken, and Jacquin's Rock and Rye. He set them on the table, opened the fridge, still standing cockeyed from when he shoved it off my mother's earring, and snagged a brown bottle of Iron City beer.

"There's the lot of it," he said, flipping off the beer cap with a church key and taking a long swig. Smoke, then foam, rose out of the bottle head when he set the beer down.

"Bourbon," she said. "Up."

My dad busted the seal and poured her a good two inches of rust. Then he emptied the full ashtray of butts into the trash, lit two Chesterfields from the pack lying on the table, and handed one to my mother.

"Thank you, Travis. You can be very sweet. But are you going to only drink beer?"

"For now."

"I got the raviolis," I said again. "They're in the living room."

"Go get them, Fritzy, and I'll heat them up," my dad said.

"Go get them, Fritzy, and I'll heat them up," my mother mimicked, then laughed and swallowed half her bourbon.

I looked at my dad.

"Go ahead, Fritzy," he said. "Mom'll feel better after she eats."

I fetched the Chef Boyardee cans and my father dumped both into a big sauce pan.

"Chef Boyardee is an impostor," my mother said. "He's no more Italian than Paddy's pig. Some fat Irish bastard who slapped on a chef's hat and a mustache."

"I'll bet you have that on the best authority," my dad came back.

"You know I'm not going to eat that slop, Travis."

"I thought that's what you were craving, Rita?"

"I want Fritzy to sit on my lap. Fritzy, are you too old to sit on your mother's lap?"

I stayed rooted in the kitchen doorway. My dad stirred the ravioli. I stared at his white blank back, the curly black hair at the back of his head. He was steeling himself with impassivity, thinking perhaps that if he didn't handle my mother properly, it would be a long hellish night. The prelude, then the thing itself: another season of silence.

"Soon I'll have a baby sitting on my lap," my mother said. I didn't know if she was talking to me or my dad. I kept my eyes on his back as he rolled the wooden spoon around the inside of the pan. "It's funny. Your baby's on your lap, then he's not. You look away, check the time or something, and he's walking, when one minute ago, he was sitting on your lap."

My dad turned from the stove and looked at my mother. He looked almost afraid. Of what, I couldn't possibly say. But it was a face he could not have made unless he loved her completely.

"This baby'll be different," she said. "We hurried you, Fritzy."

I don't know if I had ever looked into my mother's face without makeup. She had large pores and tiny pockmarks high on her cheeks. And a layer of down. Pretty brown eyes, and lush eyebrows she highlighted with pencil each night before work. The menthol smell of Noxzema. I wanted to kiss her on the cheek.

"Fritz, would you mind leaving your mother and me alone for a minute or two?" asked my dad suddenly.

"He doesn't have to leave, Travis. I'll behave myself."

"Are you ready for your dinner, Rita?"

"I thought we were going to have a little drink."

"We're having a little drink." My dad held up his beer bottle.

"I'd like Fritz to have a drink."

"Fritz is a little young to drink." He spooned some of the ravioli onto a plate, grabbed a fork, and set them in front of my mother.

"How old are you now, Fritz?" my mother asked. She had gaffed one of the stuffed little squares. The edges were pleated, the sauce yellowish. She set down the fork and took a drag of her cigarette, then killed the bourbon left in her glass.

She was joking; she knew how old I was.

"You have a very stupid look on your face, Fritz. It brings out the Sweeney in you. How old are you?"

"Lay off, Rita," my father said.

"How would you like to have a little brother or sister?" she inquired.

I looked at my mother's stomach: a little mound under her robe. I tried to look inside her. Like Superman and his X-ray vision. I concentrated. I brought to bear all my belief in the life swimming inside my mother. And for a moment, like a distant flash of heat lightning, I saw the baby, outlined in white light, like one of those little unchristened souls, neither boy nor girl, trapped in limbo. It was listening to us, peering through the womb out into our dark kitchen. Its eyes were large and gleaming.

"Do you know where babies come from, Fritz?" my mother asked.

"Come on, Rita," my father said.

I shifted my eyes from my mother to my father. He was looking at her. The beer bottle drooping from his hand at mid-thigh. Then back to my mother who had picked up her fork again.

She reached toward me with her other hand, grabbed my earlobe and gently tugged it. Then she smiled at me. The sweetest smile. That for a sliver of a second left her unguarded.

"How about if I kill myself," she said.

"Rita," my dad said. "Please, Rita. Whatever it is, let's not give in to it. Okay? Please?"

She looked at him. Still with that smile, but her eyes were scrubbed of memory, like Jersey Joe Walcott's when he came to after Marciano knocked him out for the title. My father had told me about it.

Very deliberately, looking the while into my father's paper-blue eyes, she slid the plate inch by inch to the edge of the table until it crashed to the floor.

"Thank you for the lovely dinner, Travis."

My father lit another cigarette.

"Do you really think, Travis, that you could make me pregnant? Do you think this is your baby? Do you think Fritz is yours?"

"I should rub your face in that, Rita."

"You'd have to grow some balls for that, gutless wonder."

The baby, in its chrysalis, cocked its infinitesimal blue head and listened. Then it whispered. Wordlessly. Whispered to me. Blue voice. Soundless. Whispering to me. I whispered back: *Thy womb Jesus.* I had started saying the Hail Mary to myself; I had started to cry. I bent to clean the mess, but my parents didn't notice. They stared out at the night, like strangers on a train at opposite windows. The kitchen stilled and began to fade.

My mother had already stopped speaking to us. We were dead to her. She was dead to herself. The baby rose up out of her and disappeared.

SCAFFOLD

Shotty gives me a lift to and from work every day, so I'm at his mercy if he decides to stop for a few hooches after quitting time. Tonight it's Sunset's, a dusty dark bar in Aspinwall on the way home from the town houses we're bricking out in Rowena Township.

Shotty's my Uncle Pat's fastest, best bricklayer, the Brooks Robinson of bricklayers. Pat and Shotty grew up together on the same street. Supposedly very tight. Pat was in World War II, stationed in Italy, then the Pacific islands. Fastened in a corner of my mother's vanity mirror is a picture of him in Naples, shirtless, movie-star handsome, squatting with a rifle across his haunches. She idolizes Pat, but they have little to do with each other. Whatever it is it's sealed up like those marble vaults they slide you into up at Mount Carmel. Something dead they walked away from and refused to talk about. But the dead thing's not dead. It's still clawing at the roof of the coffin, and they've known all along.

When Pat came home after V-J Day he bought a worn-out pickup and some used scaffold and became a brick contractor. Shotty was the first bricklayer he hired. Then he had the accident that ruined his legs. One afternoon, ten minutes before quitting time, Shotty was standing on moldy planks spanning a rusty buck, bricking an attic gable on a four-storey house for some doctor out in Holy Cross. He was used to the sway; it gets a little windy that high. Heights didn't bother him a bit. Then the whole damn thing collapsed like a bombed building and crashed into the site with Shotty folded up inside. Now he won't go near a scaffold. Won't even help build it. If his feet aren't on the ground, he won't lift a trowel. That's the agreement he has with Pat, who he now treats with familiarity, but hardly affection.

"One minute you're okay," Shotty says. "And the next minute you're not." He catches Lou the barkeep's eye and motions with his finger like he's hitting a typewriter key—two taps, slowly writing his story of the scaffold, one beer at a time—and Lou delivers a couple more little green bottles of Rolling Rock. I'm nursing my second with three full ones backed up in front of me. I tell Shotty I'm good, but he keeps buying them. "Tut," he says when I reach for my wallet. He leaves his money on the bartop, and Lou subtracts the tally each round.

I don't like to hear about the accident, so I don't encourage him. Shotty loves to talk about it, as if in repeating it, he's perfecting it, getting closer and closer to what really might have happened. Adding little embellishments. In one version, it was blowing a gale, the cotter pins ringing in the scaffold bucks; in another, still as church. Or he had just eaten an eggplant sandwich, worked right through lunch, ate half a pound of mortar along with the *melanzano*. Or: it was a rush job. Pat wouldn't even let them break to eat. Or: it was a Saturday in July and they had been listening to the Pirates doubleheader on some hophead black laborer's transistor. Guy named Skelton, muscle-bound, arms like big black pythons. Could stand on the ground and hoist a full hod of mud to the bricklayers working on second-storey scaffold. Was married to a white broad. Pirates were playing the Dodgers and Furillo was coming to bat. No, Campanella.

No, it was November and drizzling. Caro Melfi was digging a footer around the house they were bricking, water spilling off the roof, drenching Caro, who every few minutes took a break. Leaning on his long-handled spade, rain leaking out of his hat, when a square of shingles the roofers left slid off the roof and drove Caro's head down on the spade handle. Through his mouth, ripped out part of his throat. Dead right there in the mud. Dead as a bitch, and Pat like no big deal, screaming get back to work. Then on top of everything the scaffold, with Shotty gazing down at the impaled Caro, decides to buckle. That fucking tightwad *mamaluco* Pat. They shouldn't have been out there in that weather anyhow. Shotty cocks his head and another version pops into it like he's Aesop.

I feel bad about what happened to Shotty, but I'll start working scaffold for the first time tomorrow, and I'm scared. Every time Shotty talks about it, I see him standing there clutching his mud-loaded trowel in midair, forty, fifty feet up, suddenly with nothing under him; then he goes down like a wrecking ball, planks and brick and mortar, the steel scaffolding snarling over him and finally burying him when he hits the ground like a sack of mortar.

Then it's me, not Shotty, I see flying off the scaffold, so I clamp shut my eyes for one long second to erase it. When I open them Shotty's face is three inches from mine. He's going to drink a lot tonight. He has that loony glint in his eyes. He wants to talk about the hospital and the operations, how they nearly had to whack off one of his legs, and the pins and screws and how one leg's shorter than the other now, so he needs a stepladder to kiss a broad, how he should have sued my Uncle Pat, that penny-pinching piece of *cacca. Merda.* I know all about it. It's me, not him, I'm seeing.

I pick up my beer and take another sip, look through the bottle, through the beer, at the "33" on the back side of the Rolling Rock label.

"Hey, Shotty," I say. "What's this '33' for?"

He doesn't hesitate: "That's how old Jesus was when He died on the cross for our sins."

Then he tells me he read a survey in *Parade* magazine about drinking. Ten questions. He asks me if I think he's an alcoholic. He drinks at lunch and he keeps a Styrofoam cooler in his trunk. Little seven-ounce Rolling Rock cans. He sneaks a few in during the day here and there—"a little taste"—and he always drinks on the way home. But, as far as I can tell, he's perfectly in control at all times. I'm not much of a drinker myself, but after eight-plus hours of carrying a hod under the naked sun, it tastes good, and Sunset's has no problem serving it up to eighteen-year-olds. I don't want Shotty to think I'm not taking him seriously, so I eye him dead center. He looks like a white Sammy Davis, Jr. Exactly. I tell him I don't think he's an alcoholic—all he drinks is beer—and this seems to satisfy him. But I don't really know. I can't imagine the lives of other people.

Still, something's eating him. Shotty's son, Rocco, was killed in Vietnam: the battle of Hue in 1968. Everybody in Pat's outfit knows this, so we all keep the necessary distance from the subject. Shotty wears Rocco's gold cross around his neck, apparently all that was left of him. Today, one of the carpenters from another crew made a remark about the cross. Shotty's a genius with profanity and possesses other traits not associated with a cross. So this guy kind of flicks at the cross, just kidding, innocent, a good guy, and cracks: *What's the story? You wearing a cross?*

Shotty went nuts, dropped his trowel, tottered up on his mangled legs like he wanted to fight, shouted: *It belonged to my kid. Is that okay with you?* His chest up against this carpenter, the guy backing up and just looking at him like *What did I say?* Shotty gimping at him, shouting over and over: *Is that okay?* Until one of the other bricklayers, Ernie, stepped in and shushed him down.

The bar is dark, the only light from the neon beer signs and the Carrrara glass wall fronting the street. The shadows of people walking by on the sidewalk make little zags of light that flash off the bartop. Lou wipes a tray of wet pilsener glasses and fits them into a rack hanging from the ceiling. He wears a white long-sleeved shirt, and hums. His hair and his face are the same pasty color. There are only two other people at the bar: an old lady with a blonde wig drinking Rose and a bookie named Ray-Ray who looks like Roy Orbison, same shades too, and drinks shot after shot of vodka. They both chain smoke.

"How old are you?" Shotty asks me.

I tell him eighteen.

"My kid was twenty when he died. Twenty."

He says it like I have only two years left to live. He taps twice, and Lou yanks two more from the cooler. The blonde lady is talking to herself. I pull out a cigarette and light up, stalling before I say something to Shotty. I can feel him looking at me, as if he has a clock on me, and time's about to run out. I wish something would happen. A fire or tornado, something to propel us all into motion, to rescue us from this gloom.

But Shotty answers for me: "Damn shame, huh?"

"Yeah," I tell him. "It is a shame."

"Sent my wife to Mayview. She went instant psycho, *Christina Puzza*, like she had this other person living inside her just waiting for a catastrophe. Now the old her, the one I married, lives inside the maniac, and believe me it has plenty of room. She's big as a block truck. They pump this shit in her to keep her nerves in check and it blows her up like the Goodyear blimp. She was one outta sight broad back in the day, built like a brick shithouse. I go every Sunday, take flowers, stroll with her around the grounds like walking a Saint Bernard. She smiles and twirls her fingers in her hair, cracks her gum. Then I leave. She's still my wife, but I can't say I love her anymore. Ain't that a hell of a note?"

"Yes, it is," I say. I want to get out of this tomb and get some air, look up in the sky and see the sun still there. But Shotty has me pinned down. He's spilling like he needs to and I owe it to him to listen if he wants to talk. When I first walked on the job, he took me under his wing, did a lot of things for me he didn't have to do: transportation, lent me work boots, knew when to lay off when I was falling apart those first days from the heat and cramps and blisters. He brought me along so I can hump a day with a hod on my shoulder like the rest of the laborers. Not as good as most, but not the worst. So I offer it up and reach for the next green bottle in line.

The old lady drops off her stool and staggers out the door, mumbling and holding onto her daffodil-colored hair. A strand of light strikes Ray-Ray. He throws back another vodka and quips: "That's one sick broad, that one." Lou immediately fills his empty shot glass.

Shotty taps and Lou lays two more on us.

I get up and go to the bathroom. Directly above the trough is a rubber machine. There's a picture of a topless woman plastered on it. I stare at her the entire time I pee, take two quarters out of my pocket, stack them and fit them in the slot. The thing is in a square black and white shiny packet. Like a chimp, I rip it open and turn the lubricated rubber over and over. It smells like gasoline. I roll it down my middle finger, take it off, wrap it in toilet paper and throw it away. Then I wash my hands and walk back into the bar.

Shotty is combing his hair. Widow's peak, the goatee so sharp it looks like it was cut out and sewed on, mortar splashes around his eyes: it all makes him look in the spooky light of the bar like the devil. Ray-Ray is gone.

"I'd like to see the results if Ray-Ray completed the *Parade* survey. Son-of-a-bitch drank eighteen shots," Shotty says. "Eighteen. Right, Lou?"

"Eighteen," Lou responds. "He's a marvel."

"Me and Ray-Ray graduated from reform school together. If you can imagine this, he still lives with his mother."

"That's correct," Lou replies.

"Let's get the hell outta here," Shotty says. He asks Lou for a bag, and we load up the half dozen beers I haven't gotten to.

Shotty drives a two-door '67 gold Bonneville full of brick tools and empties, everything coated in mortar dust. It smells like the job. A Saint Christopher dangles from the rearview mirror: he carries Baby Jesus across a creek.

The Pope or somebody recently came out and said he doesn't count any more, that there was no Saint Christopher. No patron saint of travel. All those years everybody was hoping to get from here to there safely, spending money on Christopher medals and magnetized dashboard statues, they were praying to a figment. Nobody was watching over them. I saw a movie that claimed Jesus never died. The apostles gave him a drug so he'd seem dead. So he really didn't come back from the dead; he just woke up. It was a ruse to make a man God. A political plot. Power. Money. It seems more likely than the Resurrection.

I mention the Saint Christopher thing to Shotty, but he says he doesn't give a shit what the Pope says. He's sticking with Christopher. You can't revoke a saint. You have to draw the line somewhere. "Besides," he says, dropping a drained bottle on the floorboard at my feet, "belief is like a woman. You're in love with the one lying naked next to you."

We're driving across the Highland Park Bridge, high cyclone fence along the rails. The sun bobs on the river. The water cupping it looks on fire.

"There are people in that river," Shotty says. He reaches into the bag between us and cracks another beer.

I don't know what he means so I don't say anything. I stare at the water getting redder and redder.

"Dead people I'm talking about. They don't find everyone that jumps in that water. They're still under there."

"Yeah," I say.

I've always prayed in a kind of half-assed way that I'll pass through danger untouched. I believe that if I ask for protection, I can count on it. But now, looking at that long drop to the fiery river, thinking about all those dead people Shotty mentioned bumping around somewhere under the surface, I'm scared. All those times I prayed, maybe there's been no one listening. Tomorrow I'll be tightroping shaky scaffold, weighted down with a hundred pounds of slippery mud in a hod with a mind of its own, laboring for that jagoff Ted who has a hard-on for me because I'm Pat's nephew. Maybe no one will be watching over me. No Christopher. No Jesus. Who's going to hold me up?

Shotty starts singing: *Keep in mind that Jesus Christ died for us. Yes, He is our saving Lord. He is the help of all ages.* A pretty song, and Shotty does right by it.

"You know that song?" he asks.

"Uh-huh."

"They sang it at my kid's funeral. Whole damn battalion of priests. Honor guard from the 82nd Airborne. Twenty-one gun salute up Mount Carmel. It was something else."

We're in East Liberty now, and it's just about dark. The Bonneville rattles along Highland Avenue and I'm feeling the four beers I drank. All that's left now is to go home to the empty house, eat whatever my dad fixed for me before he and my mother left for the night shift, then crawl into bed. One minute I'm okay; the next minute I'm not. That scaffold's in my head. First it's Shotty going down. Then his son, Rocco, gets blown into the sky. Then it's me. Up there frozen. Looking down at the indifferent world for the last time before the hod drags me off the ragged plank.

"You hungry?" Shotty asks.

"Yeah. I guess."

"Tell you what. Let's swing by my house and I'll cook supper. You okay with that?"

Shotty lives in a tiny house on Auburn Street. Like a little box: three rooms and a bathroom. It's immaculate, fastidious, like the whole place was put together with a T square and a slide rule.

"What?" Shotty says. "You think there were going to be piles of sand and busted bricks all over the place? I know how to keep house. Here." He hands me a beer. "Make yourself at home. I'm going to take a quick shower. Chip some of this shit offa me."

One wall of the living room is a shrine to Rocco. There's a photograph of him and three other guys in combat fatigues. Rifles and helmets. Smiling like crazy. All four of them. Something familiar about Rocco's smile. Then another picture of just him in his dress uniform with epaulets and a necktie, one of those hats like cops wear pulled down over his eyebrows, chiseled jaw, his mouth a slash across it. No turning away from the shit about him. It scares me to look at him. What he went through. There's a flag in a shadow box, folded into a triangle, and a little cabinet displaying his medals. A dozen at least. The only one I recognize is the Purple Heart. On a pedestal under Rocco's picture is a red votive candle on a white saucer. The wick is black and streams of dried wax fan over the plate. I think of the scaffold and want to run out of Shotty's house and never stop.

Shotty comes up behind me carrying a colander and a Rolling Rock. He wears a fresh V-necked white T-shirt like the dirty one he changed out of, the gold cross widowed in his silver chest hair, a pair of khaki shorts, and bedroom slippers. I've never seen him so clean. Suddenly I feel weighted with grime and stench.

"That's Rocco."

"Yeah," I say. A stupid thing to say. I want to tell Shotty how sorry I am. I want to throw my arms around him. Now would be the time to do it. But all I do is whisper "yeah" again.

He hands me the colander. "How about stepping out in the back and picking some lettuce. I eat a salad every night. Very good for you."

I just look at him.

"Fritz, are you awake? Go out to the garden and pick a little lettuce. You know what lettuce looks like?"

Shotty's yard backs up to a gravel alley where little black kids play kickball under the streetlight. The yard's no bigger than a confessional, but the whole thing's planted in peppers, lettuce, eggplant, zucchini, and tomato plants with small, star-shaped yellow flowers on them. He even has two rows of corn almost as tall as me. In the middle of the garden is a bench and a gray statue of Saint Francis. A bird sits in his hand and another on his shoulder. The top of his head is shaved, and he wears a goatee. From the side he looks like Shotty.

I fill the colander with lettuce, sit on the bench, and smoke a cigarette. It's dark except for the streetlight. The kids sing out as they play, darting over the gravel in bare feet. I can make out people on the porches across the alley. Their voices float over to me. And charcoal smoke. These are the long nights.

Shotty's at the stove working away. It smells good in the kitchen. His legs fall out of his shorts and dangle above the floor. The left is straight as an angle iron, pitifully spindly, no calf. The other, the short one, bows out, the kneecap plopped cockeyed on the side of his leg. Both are pocked and striated with blue scars.

We sit down and Shotty mumbles a rapid-fire grace. We both make the sign of the cross. "Help yourself," he says. He's made pastina and eggs, a dish I love, but have forgotten. My grandmother, I think, used to make it for me when I was a baby.

Pastina and eggs is like mortar, Shotty tells me. There's an art to mixing it. It can't be too stiff or too soupy. It has to be just right. And you have to use baby pastina. Three eggs, not two. And Pecorino Romano. Period. Some things you can't compromise on. I eat two plates of it. Shotty passes me Italian bread and salad, gets up and brings me a beer.

"I want to tell you something," he says.

I look up from eating. Shotty's staring at me. He's smiling. He lays down his fork, and takes a drink of beer.

"My kid, Rocco, he was in Vietnam in 1968."

"I know," I say in what I hope is a soothing voice.

"Whatta you know?" His voice has an edge, a challenge. "Whatta you know?" he says again, like he's getting pissed. "You don't know what I want to tell you."

"No, I don't know that at all."

"Rocco was in Vietnam for one year. In the middle of serious shit. Wounded at the battle of Hue, back at the front in six weeks. All that shit on the wall is real. That's him. His medals, the flag they handed me before they dropped him in the ground."

Wounded at the battle of Hue? Rocco was killed at the battle of Hue. I look at Shotty like my mind's blown. He's getting worked up, like today with the carpenter. That's what this is all about. If I can just look at him and keep my mouth shut, if I can listen perfectly to him, and not think about tomorrow and the scaffold, then he'll get to the other side of this, whatever it is he wants to say, and we'll both be okay.

"Rocco made it home, Fritz."

I'm looking at him as hard as I can, trying to make my face look like a plaster saint's face. A face you can tell anything to.

Shotty kind of smiles. He can see I'm shocked. Rocco didn't die at Hue after all. He made it out of Vietnam. To Camp Pendleton in California. After discharge, he decided to stay out there and go to school on the GI Bill. But that was bullshit. He never went to school. He had a secret life. Everything he told Shotty and his wife was made up. They thought he was going to school, but he grew a beard and long hair and spent his days wasted. Some kind of hippie. They discovered all this later when Shotty flew to California to claim the body. Rocco had been dead for a few days, sitting there in a pile of expensive dope in front of one TV show after another, before the landlord found him. Shotty says he didn't recognize Rocco; he was so fat.

"A big fat bag of shit," Shotty cracks, and I see how fried he is over it, making fun of his dead kid, but not really. "Fat, Fritzy. I mean gargantuan. Six people. Just like my old lady. What the fuck? I'm fading away, and everybody around me's like that thing, the blob, in the Steve McQueen movie."

Shotty refused the autopsy. There was no sign of foul play. The coroner figured cardiac arrest: this big fat guy just pushing it way harder than he could handle. *Natural causes.* At twenty! Shotty smiles and takes a long pull from his beer. "I didn't want to know nothing about it. Did I have to know what it was inside his body that assassinated him? Like that would have mattered? Like that would have made some sense to me? Did I have to know that?"

He looks at me like he wants an answer. I tell him hell no, he was right to leave that part of it alone. His kid was dead, his wife in Mayview. What else is there after that?

"Fucking A," Shotty says. He confesses that the lie about Rocco zapped at Hue just came to him. It was the easiest thing to do. The real Rocco story was complicated, difficult to understand. The Vietnam Rocco, the one on the wall, told its own story, no questions asked. People hung their head, put an arm around him, and walked away. "I was ashamed too," he says. "So I buried him out there—my wife was a zombie—and then I lied. And now I'm telling you. I'm telling you, Fritzy. The truth."

I nod. For Shotty. A nod that says it's okay, I understand, forget about it. It's what I know to do. My own lie. Nobody tells the truth.

Even so, Shotty's holding out on me. There's way more to this story: Rocco, the wife in Mayview. Shotty's conspicuously left himself out of the whole equation. Like he might not have had anything to do with it. As if he were outside of it all. Just a concerned citizen mopping up.

But so what if there's more? He's cooked up a story he can live with. One everybody else can live with. Maybe he beat his wife. Maybe he beat the kid. Did horrible dark satanic things guaranteed to produce tragedy.

Shotty could've said to me: "The deal about Rocco dying in front of the TV. Pure bullshit. Yes, he was a fat motherfucker dopehead with a heart condition at twenty, but you know how he died? You want to know?"

And I would have told him to shut up, that I'm scared shitless about the scaffold tomorrow, and it's starting to sound like he's talking about me, not Rocco. I don't even know that I believe there ever was a Rocco. Shotty could have bought the pictures and flag and medals at the Army-Navy store downtown on Liberty Avenue. I would have told him, hell no, I don't want to know. I want you to shut your mouth.

But he'd go on nevertheless. Rocco didn't die in front of the TV, but running from the cops. His war hero kid after he kicked in a drug store window and couldn't even get the cash register open. Or maybe he shook down an old lady for her empty handbag. His war hero kid—no fight, no shoot-out—just keeled and croaked, there on the sunny sidewalks of paradise 3,000 miles from home. Too fat to even run from the cops.

In another version, Shotty admits that he hadn't talked to Rocco in months, that he had kind of disowned his son. He doesn't know. He starts to cry. Stammers out through the veil of his hands: "Fat fuck." I don't know how to approach Shotty. Here he is, weeping, I mean weeping, like Saint Peter after he sold Jesus down the river. "Jesus Christ," he's wailing, raking his hands through his hair, tears tracking through the hair on his arms, dripping off his elbows to the green and orange flowered linoleum, and maybe a black woman comes to the door of his back porch. Two little children, a boy and a girl, trail her like acolytes. The alley streetlight floods them in light. Far off, a siren wails. I kneel beside Shotty and put my hand on his shoulder. He continues to weep, brings one of his hands up and lays it on mine. Or he throws it off and tells me to get the fuck out of his house. What do I know about suffering? What do I know about anything?

"Get your black asses off my porch," he screams at the woman and children.

Who knows? Rocco might not have been fat at all. He might have been skinny. Like his old man. That makes more sense. Shotty probably doesn't weigh a hundred and ten pounds. He looks like a sliver of flint patched with pipe cleaners.

Shotty's kid could have been in Montreal, dodging the draft.

Take your pick. There are multiple versions of everything.

Pat probably knows the real story, but he doesn't seem to believe in the past at all. He doesn't even remember that I'm his nephew. He claims Shotty never fell off one of his scaffolds, but was drunk one night and rolled off the top of a bunk bed in a South Side flophouse right out a second-storey window. Pat laughs when he says this, but it's more of a sneer. I think my mother knows what really happened, but she's too superstitious about dead children to talk with any real depth about Rocco, other than to say it was a shame and that she heard he was a drinker like his old man—what can you expect?—and that he got in with the wrong crowd. The apple doesn't fall too far from the tree. While she's talking, she shoots my dad a look that's unmistakable: Rocco, whatever happened, is something they long ago agreed not to talk about. All she'll allow is that Shotty's an operator who can find the back entrance to every bar in Pittsburgh in his sleep. His real name is Basil, but the wife, she says, is news to her. My father doesn't say a word.

I think I remember Rocco. Curly black hair, big gap between his two front teeth, thin and tallish, muscular, tan girlish beauty. I guess I had been seeing him, like Shotty, all my life, but had never really noticed him. He and his dog, Skeeter, a black and white spotted mutt with the temperament of a Benedictine, that was always with him. Who came like Lassie or Rin Tin Tin whenever Rocco whistled for him.

Rocco showed up one day, out of nowhere, it seemed, carrying two hoops, nets, and a basketball. Borrowed a ladder from the Paganos across the street and with his dad's brick hammer nailed the hoops to the naked backboards that had been hanging at opposite ends of the Dilworth school yard, waiting for Rocco to complete them, since I could remember. He threaded the lacy white nets to the bright orange steel. Then he genuflected to the red cobblestone floor, picked up the ball and started shooting.

For the first time ever there was the sound of dribbling in the school yard, rims chiming and the chant of the net every time Rocco fired it through from way out. I swear to God the nets fluttered when he walked by them. Balls hung in the air spinning on invisible fingers.

Kids came from all over East Liberty. Played all day; all night, in the high beams of idling junkers, the radios cued to the FM underground station: Iron Butterfly, Cream, Buffalo Springfield, Big Brother and the Holding Company, Jefferson Airplane, guys in cutoffs and high Stars gliding up and down the court.

Occasionally, I played, but wasn't much good. Sometimes in the early morning I'd catch Rocco there alone, except for Skeeter, lying on the cool slick cobblestones, front paws extended, his head resting on them, his eyes on Rocco. Rocco would invite me to shoot with him, taking the time to coach me: spin, arc, velocity, release. We'd play Twenty-one, Horse, Tips. He hummed "Down on Me," sang songs from *Revolver.* Wore an army jacket, let his hair and beard grow, which made him even darker. Che Guevara. Gave me some skin every time I sunk one. As the sun rolled its way up the roof of Dilworth School, the others would arrive in ones and twos and I'd bow out, content to sit on the step and watch and smoke cigarettes.

Black kids from the projects across the Hollow came to play, then others filtered over the Meadow Street Bridge from the ghettoes off Larimer Avenue. Everybody was nervous, but Rocco knew quite a few of them—he lived on the other side of the bridge—shook their hands and introduced them around. Everything was cool. Just pickup games. Detente: dialogue through hoops, like sign language. Even so, the families up and down Saint Marie Street were uneasy. They didn't like the black kids hanging around; they didn't like those all-night games, the bright lights and the music.

Girls, too, black and white, had taken to hanging around the school yard during the night games: the smell of marijuana wafting along Saint Marie like frankincense, the hoopers, like X-rays sweating phosphorus in the parked cars' brights, Rocco, now in the raiment of Aquarius, climbing a carpet of night light to lay it up. And the music thunderclapping from the dashboards—*We got to get together sooner or later because the revolution's here*—the girls' long hair, the Afros. Rocco Montesanto, Shotty's kid: turncoat, half *tizzone.*

One night the cops came and ran everybody out, threw a couple of the black guys over the boiling hoods of their cruisers and searched them. The next morning the hoops were gone. Just the twisted nails that had held them writhing out of the backboards. And Skeeter had been run over. Rocco never stopped smiling. He smoked cigarettes, a little dope, threw the I Ching and read Thomas Mann. But there was less and less of him, like he was crossing over. The last time I saw him—1966, maybe '67, a year or so before Hue—he had a copy of *The Magic Mountain* under his arm. Then he disappeared, saw clean through to the other side, like some of those far-out kids in East Liberty back then, prophets and junkies and poets, and stepped through the portal. Sucked up in a beam of alien light. Caught a bum draft number. Played Icarus for one scorched instant off the Meadow Street Bridge. No telling what really happened. I think of that almost panicked look between my mother and father when I asked them about Rocco. That's where he is: in the enduring breach of silence and forgetfulness, East Liberty's eighth sacrament. In the tiny flame of that votive Shotty lights for him every night.

I'm satisfied not knowing the truth. Falsehood is often all we have. Lies spare you. They keep you alive, moving course to course, storey to storey, job to job. The scaffold is that shaky construct: truth. It can collapse upon you at any time. For all I know, what Shotty just told me is bullshit. But those busted-up legs he drags around on aren't bullshit. I don't think his regret and sorrow are bullshit either. Still, what I want of all these versions is Rocco dead in Vietnam, vaporized, a hero. Not like me or Shotty.

Now he's just like any other East Liberty loser. But that's okay too.

"How's your food?" Shotty asks.

"Very good."

"You want some more?"

"No, I'm fine. Thanks."

Shotty gets up, limps over and turns on TV. The Pirates are playing the Cincinnati Reds. He's still drinking beer. He turns the TV off, comes back and starts clearing dishes from the table. He asks me if I want another beer, but I'm finished, up to here with everything.

"What I told you, Fritz, about Rocco. It's not a lie. It's a secret." I grab a couple of dishes and carry them to the sink, pondering the difference between a secret and a lie. The distinction is lost on me. It's late. Tomorrow's another working day. The scaffold steals over me black as the night outside Shotty's. Danger. Fear. Cowardice. I want to talk to Shotty about it: my secret. My lie. But his head is crammed full of his own story.

"I better get going, Shotty. Thanks for everything." I head for the door.

"I'll drive you."

"Nah, that's okay. I'm going to walk."

"You not worried about all those brothers out there?"

"I'll be okay."

"I'll pick you up in the morning."

"Okay. See ya."

"So you don't think I'm an alcoholic then?" he asks after I'm already outside.

"No," I say through the screen door.

"Good. I don't have to worry about that then. I'll check it off my list."

The second I step off Shotty's little stoop, the door shuts and the lock clicks. Most of the lights in the houses up and down the street are out. It's not a long walk, but it's dark as hell. I smoke cigarettes the whole way. I'm going to give them up, I tell myself every time I strike a match and pull a gust into my lungs.

There's the scaffold and Shotty's kid and there's Shotty. But mostly it's me. Up on the scaffold. And I'm scared. Each time I pass a gang of black guys angling out of the night at me. For a moment I don't think I can go on. Then I decide I want to hurry everything, get it over with. I run the last few blocks. I'll take a shower, get to bed, and tomorrow I'll stagger up the scaffold with hods of brick and mortar while Ted screams at me to hurry it the fuck up.

The house is black when I get home. Not one light left on. Not even the porch light. No note. I turn on all the lights. My food's in the oven in a plate under aluminum foil. I take it out and put it in the refrigerator. I walk through the house looking for signs of my parents' love for me. But all I see is what passes for their routine: the unmade bed; ashtrays salted with cigarette butts; the ironing board with the iron and half a cup of coffee on it; my mother's curlers on the bathroom sink, strands of her bleached yellow hair wiring out of them; a wet towel wadded on the floor.

What would they do if I died? If Pat appeared at the door and announced that I had fallen four stories off one of his crummy scaffolds? My mother would run around tearing at her hair screaming, "Oh, my God." My father would walk quietly into the kitchen and sit at the table for the rest of his life. Maybe one of them would go crazy. They would not comfort each other. My name would not pass between them ever again. In time, they would construct a fine and durable lie to conceal my unremarkable life and death. A wall of the living room would be devoted to me.

I turn on the TV, sit down in front of it, and wait for them. They won't be home until three, maybe later.

ZEPPOLE

My mother swears she's pregnant. She wants to cook. Which she never does. In our house, my father handles the cooking. As recently as yesterday she wasn't even speaking to us, but this baby—*the baby*, she says—has her happy and she wants to make *zeppole.* Little patties of dough fried in hot olive oil, then sprinkled with sugar. She has a craving. The way her mother used to make them. I don't remember ever eating them, but my mother assures me I have. At my grandmother's. But we hardly see her any more, and I'm not certain I'd recognize her if she crashed through the roof.

My mother produces a white prayer book with a tiny lock like an antique diary's. With a key the size of an infant's thumbnail she opens it. Should she drop to her knees, mumbling antiphonies like those insane Calabrian widows on Good Fridays at the graveyard, I will fall over dead in astonishment, and my father will join me. But she does not pray. Rather, she takes from the prayer book's withered secret pages a slip of frayed paper and, reading from it as she puffs on a Chesterfield, assembles the grayish-yellow mound of dough.

My father sits reading the obituaries at the kitchen table. Wearing a long white terry cloth robe with a black hex sign on the back, he looks like a prize fighter. He tells my mother that Philly Decker died and is laid out at Febraro's.

"Did somebody shoot him or did he just eat himself to death?" she asks.

"Doesn't mention," says my dad.

"I thought he was too in love with himself to die. How will the world keep spinning?"

"I think we should go see him, Rita."

"You go. I never liked him, but please tell him I said hello."

"Your mother has no respect for the dead, Fritz," he says to me. "Or for the living."

He gets up and takes the newspaper into the living room. I follow him, lie on my stomach on the floor with the comics and doze off. As I sleep, the dough, hunkered in a glass bowl covered with a tea towel, miraculously doubles in size.

When I wake, I walk toward the kitchen. My mother, in a pink summer nightgown, stands at the ironing board running the steaming wedge back and forth across the collar of the black dress she'll wear to work. The iron occasionally hisses. From the radio, volume hiked way up, Elvis Presley, in a whispery voice, sings "I Can't Help Falling in Love with You."

She sings along as she irons, fervently, churchy, then sways, guided by Elvis over the dance floor of dream. She has not noticed me. There are tears in her eyes. Behind her, like excelsior, sun sprays the window, silhouetting her, the gown chiseled in relief, her hair spun at her crown in filigrees, her face a marbled shadow of backlight out of which drifts a disembodied yearning not clearly my mother's. And for that instant I am blinded and do not see until the sun flares off the Pentecostal flames from the ignited oil in the skillet raging behind her.

"Mom," I scream. She looks up surprised and smiles, still singing unabashedly: *Take my hand, take my whole life too.*

Then she turns and sees the fire licking at her. She grabs the wooden skillet handle. The flames leap from the skillet to her gown, pour over it like liquid, and she is instantly engulfed. The music like requiem, Elvis Presley like the cantor at High Mass looping incense over his mesmerized flock as the church burns down. I can't move. I can't take my eyes off her, no longer my mother, like sacred art restored, an angel wedding fire.

My father storms by me and scoops up my mother. He kicks open the screen door. There is an audible suspiration as he too catches fire, stumbling down the three concrete steps to the yard where he drops her, still clutching the spouting skillet, in my swimming pool, then simply steps out of his fiery robe and leaps into the water beside her.

The pool has sat in the little yard all winter. Leaves float on its surface. Neighborhood dogs drink out of it. The blue plastic bottom, patterned with yellow cartoon fish with long-lashed eyes and huge puckered lips, is slick with algae. The round aluminum frame is caving.

Unharmed, my mother and father sit next to each other in the pool. Laughing. She in what's left of the charred pink gown. Bit by bit it falls off her body and floats on the water like scraps of flesh. My father is naked. Together they splash water on his burning robe until the flames die down, and there is the sodden smell of fried terry cloth, the nubs at the end of each thread brown on white like blackened marshmallows.

THE SCHOOL FOR THE BLIND

And Jacob was left alone,
and there wrestled a man with him
until the breaking of the day.
—GENESIS 32:24

During the week leading up to our match with the School for the Blind, Brother Coach made us wear blindfolds to practice. An object lesson in piety, he claimed: discover what it's like to be deprived of sight. Saint Sebastian's was, after all, he reminded, a Christian institution. He also mandated we attend school blindfolded, scratching class to class with white, red-tipped wooden canes among the scoffing student body of 1,200 Catholic boys. If we cheated with the blindfolds, he vowed he'd pluck our eyes out.

I was fourteen years old, a small, stringy, nearly hairless freshman, with a voice still embarrassingly soprano. I wrestled the 88-pound class, even though my normal weight was 106. To make weight, I fasted like an Old Testament ascetic. I lived by the mirror, carried in my book bag a bathroom scale, weighed my spit and urine and excrement. Hungry every minute of every day, I dreamt about food.

The prospect of wrestling a blind boy terrified me.

My father liked the blindfold idea. He didn't invest much in Christian piety, but felt like a jolt in the shoes of the other guy was always enlightening. Blindness, he offered, remained the greatest affliction. My mother said she thought it stupid, that Brother could pay the hospital bill when I fell down a flight of Sebastian's long marble stairs and split my head open. She was the one who had convinced me to go out for wrestling. It would be a way for me to protect myself—like boxing, like those costumed beasts who beat the shit out of each other on *TV Studio Wrestling*. Real wrestling, however, did not permit brawling. You couldn't lock your hands or make a fist. You couldn't lift your opponent off the mat. No atomic drops, body slams, or Indian death chops. Even headlocks were illegal. She, not my father, always tried to make a man of me. She felt strongly that a boy needed a sport. My father liked sports well enough, but he didn't care about them any more than anything else. He wasn't out to prove anything. My mother constantly reproved him for this, and worried that I didn't have enough fight in me to get ahead in life.

I found out what getting ahead is once I went out for wrestling. It's about fear. And cruelty. For me there were two fears. The first was elemental: simply the fear of slapping on a uniform and placing myself apart, setting myself up the instant I set foot on the mat. I had never liked calling attention to myself. Safe distance from any kind of scrutiny appealed to me much more than notoriety. I sat in the back of my classroom, and never raised my hand nor volunteered information.

My parents both left for work every day well before I returned from school and then wrestling practice. They worked six days a week, and never made it home until the early hours of morning. Sundays we spent mostly together, but only after they finally made it out of bed late in the day. I faced little in the way of accountability. I would not have admitted how I felt if my life depended on it. In truth, I didn't know how I felt. What I most desired was invisibility.

While the first fear made me merely anxious, the second fear, the fear of losing, paralyzed me. Of walking to the middle of the mat and shaking hands with a boy who in nearly every way was my double: same exact weight, height, same age, baby-faced, petite, in the throes of puberty, another freshman in all likelihood. Our heavyweight, John DeRiso, a 238-pound senior who also played football, called the 88s *castratos,* malignant dwarves. I began to see, in the narcosis that starving engenders, my opponent as myself, actually my better self, the confident well-fed kid who strides onto the mat from a parallel universe, and ceremonially kicks my head in in front of everybody.

This is what it's like: Brother hums "Blue Moon" while he lifts you off the floor and cracks your back. The snap of your spine echoes through the gym, and suddenly you're cold, trembling. He presses his forehead to yours—his eyes are Della Robbia blue, the forehead of a basset hound—and tells you, *Take him, Sweeney.* In the middle of the mat you shake hands with your opponent, and make the mistake of looking in his face. Always beautiful, the boy who beats you, like an apparition, an angel you could have been had you not been so unworthy.

You're famished, exhausted. You've spent two tournament nights, three overtime periods too many crouping bloody hawkers into the matside bucket after outlasting some other starveling who finally fainted and all you had to do was lie on top of him and try not to black out yourself. The whole time all you think of, like forbidden pictures of women, saying Hail Marys to yourself at the same time, is the food you'll rip into after the match: pastry, ice cream. Your evil infantile lust for sugar. You're crazy. You need help: a priest, a psychiatrist.

Only a week before you beat this very boy, locked him in a cradle for the last minute and a half, but couldn't pin him. Tonight he wants you in the most inconsolable way. No one, before you, had ever taken him. His nerves are shot; he smells of Iron City and Romilar. But so are yours: vertigo, the shakes, the teeth-grinding desire for a cigarette. More than anything you want it all over with.

It takes but that instant of doubt. He reads your mind like tarot, peers deeper into your heart than your confessor: every drop of sacristy Tokay you've filched and drunk, the affronts against purity, your filthy mouth, the near occasion of sin that is your gutless raiment. You know he has you, has cast the eyes, the *malocchio*, on you as surely as Graziella, the neighborhood *strega.*

It's so sudden, even cliché, to call this loss, but it's you, on your back, the gym rafter lights leering down, car beams hurtling through the windshield, the ref on his belly sliding his hand between the mat and your shoulder blade, and finding no grace there, sounding his palm down like a round from a sniper's M16.

You try to get it through your head—*loss*—looking down at your chest where your soul had been and finding a hole, crying, Brother Coach singing very softly, *I saw you standing alone.* The ref hoists the other boy's hand. Brother lumbers out to walk you, now really falling apart, back to the bench—he knows you punked—and still you're thinking of the sweets you'll wolf like a last meal. Because you aren't tough enough.

This was my waking nightmare, so real sometimes that when it seized me, I'd forget where I was, even who I was, and it would take me a moment when finally it faded to return to the real world. And there I'd be: gobbling Ex-Lax, spitting off a pound or two into a mason jar, shoving a fist down my throat to puke, always suffocated by that rubber suit, upstairs in my bedroom skipping rope, running in place, my parents gone to their night jobs, the ductwork shimmying behind the Sheetrock with each footfall. Waiting for my blood sugar to plummet, the dehydration to set in, so I could pass out for a few hours' sleep in the scary, empty house until my cramping muscles twitched me awake, and I would cock an ear for my father's rumbling snore. But more often than not it would be the great black breath of silence drubbing the walls, my parents off in some speakeasy with an unbroken chain of nightcaps awaiting them.

Sexual longing was not even an option. A starveling wrestler, a weight-loss freak, if he's doing his job, is not simply unable to achieve erection; his glands dry up, thus his desire. A conspiracy between physiology and Calvinism. The upperclassmen would route skin rags through the locker room like pep pills, but nobody had the stomach for girls. Centerfolds enervated me. I felt nothing for them but veneration. Crying and masturbation were the same things: arid sobbing spasms, self-indulgences which, after sweating out seven pounds (you didn't have to lose to begin with) in a practice without even a swallow of water, meandered away from your conscious mind like an amnesiac's. I knew also plenty of wrestlers whose hair fell out, who developed sudden aversions to heights and closed spaces, muttered to themselves, though thank God none of those things happened to me. I did, however, become a sleepwalking, nightmaring insomniac; and also, for exactly one week during the season, I contemplated hurling myself off the Meadow Street Bridge. I wanted to tell my parents about this urge—I never conceived of it as putting an end to my life—but they were so seldom home. Often, when I did see them, the energy and will to assemble a string of coherent declarative sentences was beyond me. I felt too sorry for my parents to assault them with my own troubles.

There was a perpetual unsaid smoldering between them. Some apocalyptic secret like a thawing corpse at the bottom of their glacial booze glasses. Like they were sipping shrapnel. They had been trying for years to have a baby—my mother had been obsessed over it—and things hadn't worked out. Now they seemed to inhabit the emptiness of the baby's failure to arrive. During wrestling season I saw them only on Saturdays before they left for work and on Sundays, their only day off. They'd haul out of bed late, usually past three, and regardless of the time, my dad cooked bacon, eggs, home fries, toast. Made a big deal about it. Breakfast. My mother hunkered over a cup of coffee, wisecracking to herself, sour and disillusioned, as if my father, whistling "Lemon Tree" or "You Always Hurt the One You Love," fixed breakfast at four o'clock in the afternoon only to mock her. Whatever magic she eked out of hostessing in a go-go joint every night faded with the sun. She looked spent, haggard, her silky robe open. Maybe a slip underneath, sometimes nothing. She'd pull it across her stomach and chest, but if it fell open, so what. Her eye makeup had bled; face gray, hair like burnt grass. One match and she'd go up like tinder, taking the house, all of us, with her.

"Whatta you so happy about?" she challenged my father.

"Happy to be married to a queen like you, Rita."

"Yeah, my ass."

"Your ass is right, sweetheart. How do you want your eggs?"

"I hate eggs."

"Since when?"

"Since now."

"Then I'll fix you something else."

"Just toast."

"Coming up."

I sat at the table drinking black coffee, feeling the jags coming on as the caffeine streaked through me. By that time, a few days before the match, I had taken to wearing a blindfold at home.

"Are you going to eat something, Fritzy?" my mother asked.

"Maybe a grapefruit."

"Eat something. You look like death warmed over."

"Thanks, Mom."

"You need to eat. You're going to get sick. Do you want to get sick?"

"Rita, give the kid a break. He's in training."

"Training for what? The concentration camp? Tell him he needs to eat, Travis."

The smell of eggs and bacon had me choked up, like I was listening to the national anthem and sitting in the blue seats in right field at Forbes Field, the home-team Pirates already stationed at their positions, black caps covering their hearts. My tear ducts were bone dry, but I cried anyway. It was the food. I sat on the vinyl seat of my chair and tried to keep still.

"Jesus Christ," my mother said. "He acts like he's having some kind of fit."

After wrestling practice, the day before the match with the School for the Blind, I'm slumped at the yellow counter of Rudy's House of Submarines on Murray Avenue in Squirrel Hill, a good ways from my own neighborhood. A miraculous two pounds under—eighty-six pounds of gristle—I order a mushroom-cheese-steak and a chocolate milk shake. The cook drops shaved strips of pink steak on the greasy grill. He throws on a big handful of mushrooms and scrambles it up with his spatula. As they writhe and sizzle he splits open a foot-long hoagy roll with a butcher knife, lays three squares of white American cheese on the steak and mushrooms until they melt, scrapes the whole mess off the grill, tucks it in the bread, loads it with lettuce, tomato, and onion, oil and vinegar, splits the sub with one swipe of the blade, plops it before me on a paper plate, then delivers the milk shake.

My hunger is obscene. I have never eaten anything that has tasted so much of sheer joy and damnation simultaneously. I can't quite believe it. When I'm finished with the sandwich, I order another. Every crumb, every shred of lettuce, and tomato seed I consume. I lick the delicious soggy plates, run my finger inside the milk shake cup and suck my fingers. I drop off the stool and walk next door into Iz Cohen's Deli, buy a corned beef sandwich, a wedge of cheesecake, and four Chunky candy bars to go. I sit on the high city curb outside and gorge through it, intending next to cross the street and top it all off with two cuts of pepperoni pizza and a cherry Coke from Mineo's.

It's black winter now, middle of January, no turning back from anything. Snow peening down. When I spit on the telephone pole next to me, it freezes on contact. The food is so thrilling I cry smoky invisible tears, stare at the hoary bearded rabbis, robed in black and rocking on the bus islands; the yarmulkeed students, books flapping as they run to catch the bus. Shop owners pull their shades as an invisible sun skids off Murray Avenue. The world is like a strange foreign movie coaxing me farther and farther from my starving wrestler's life back in East Liberty.

Then I am suddenly back in it. Panicked. What have I done? *Jesus Lord Christ.* I'll never make weight tomorrow. Never. I can feel it in the scales of my astonished stomach. In a few moments of gluttony, I've gained, probably, five or six pounds. That's the way it works, the checks and balances of the hunger artist so precisely calibrated that a mouthful of water can cost a quarter pound, a piece of bread a half pound easy, what I've just shoved down, unthinkable, maybe more than seven or eight pounds. Brother will kill me.

I rush into the alley behind the row of restaurants and punch my hand down my throat. I throw up until I am raw with dry heaves. Instead of taking the bus, I run the five miles home, toting my school books and dirty wrestling clothes, falling again and again on the snow-coated icy sidewalks, my school shoes sodden, blistering my feet, the falling snow tearing into me. When I finally make it to the empty house, it's nine o'clock. I strip and hit the bathroom scales. Four pounds over, add an extra pound for unreliability. Five pounds. *Mother, dear God.*

I suit up: two T-shirts, jock, socks, and shorts; then the heavy rubber long-sleeved jacket and leggins, still nasty with that day's practice. With white adhesive tape, I seal the wrist and leg ends to keep the sweat from flooding out. Over the rubber suit, a pair of gray sweatpants and a hooded gray sweatshirt, tug on white high-top All Stars, tie the hood tight around my head, adjust my blindfold, then jack up the furnace full throttle. For the next hour and a half, until I am faint and nauseous, I skip rope over the heat register and turn the radio to KQV. "Ferry Cross the Mersey," "Satisfaction," "My Girl," "This Diamond Ring," my favorite songs, hurtle at me. If sorrow could smelt off flesh, I'd be ten under. I would disappear. With my eyes tied off the music shakes the house; my heart beats off the walls. The world swirls about me in vectors of yellow and red, and finally I collapse on the register, lie there shaking as I baste blind in a bag of my own runoff.

I crawl to the stairs and scutter up on hands and knees, peel off the blindfold, step into the bathtub, stop the drain and undo the tape. Water gushes out of my sleeves and cuffs. I remove each article of clothing, wring every drop of water from the sweats, T-shirts, shorts, socks, and jock, even my shoes. Enough gray sweat to bathe in. With a measuring cup I bail the tub—*one, two, three*—emptying each into the sink—*four, five, six, seven.* Twelve cups in all. Ninety-six ounces. Six pounds. Which should put me a pound under. Gingerly, I mount the scales. Ninety pounds. A wave of vertigo breaks over me. My mouth fills with copper. I step down, take a deep breath, blow it out, hold my breath and remount the scale. Eighty-nine and a half, maybe three quarters. I repeat this half a dozen times, praying that the numbers will divinely register eighty-eight, please, even eighty-nine. In the bathroom mirror I catch myself, the striae of my ribs, the knobs of my collarbone jibbing sharply in relief against the shadowy wall, my black-eyed, panicked refugee face. I am still nearly two pounds over. With a match tomorrow.

I chew up sixteen tablets of milk of magnesia, weigh the calories of those chalky white pellets against what they'll squeeze out of my intestines. I take a shower, grab an empty Contadina tomato paste can out of the garbage, sit in front of the TV and spit into the jagged steel mouth. Too dried up to spit, all I grind out is a few ounces of scurf.

The Twilight Zone: an episode about a Confederate spy about to be hanged from the Owl Creek Bridge at dawn. There is the protracted wait for the sun to break the bleak horizon, close-up of the condemned bearded man's face in a cold sweat, his horrible blazing eyes, the exaggerated theatrical tom-tom of his heart—time growing shorter—then the screech of dawn and over he goes. But, inexplicably, the rope snaps and he hits the water, the camera taking me under with him, so, naturally, I hold my breath as he sinks clear to the bottom, somehow untrussing his hands and feet, kicking off his boots, then the interminable swim to the surface. Deprived so long of oxygen, I begin to lose consciousness; my stomach knots with cramps. To drown is a peaceful death, I've heard. One simply acquiesces. A body is, after all, mostly water.

When he breaches there comes his awful suck of air that jolts me back to life, my guts twisted by the overdose of laxatives. Now in the water swimming downstream, escaping from the Yankee musket fire, miniballs cutting the water like cottonmouths mere inches from his face. Finally beached, up and running barefoot through the gorse and brake. Then a long road leading to regal wrought iron gates that swing wide of their own accord. A woman approaches from the plantation house. Smiling. Angelically beautiful. *Abby*, he calls as he races to her, the film slowing now, dilating the moment, devolving into slow motion. His face. Her face. *Abby*. Their arms extended to embrace. *Abby*. He's home. Beloved. *Abby*. The film freezing them into statuary, mere renditions; and then: the film spirits back to where he hangs, swaying solemnly at the end of the rope like an integer spliced into the risen sun.

I sprint upstairs and sit on the toilet as my guts rush out. Most of the night, it seems, boiling, convulsing under the judgmental fluorescent lights, doubled with cramps, my cheek against the cool white tile wall. Seeing that man swept out of his hallucination, collared by the rope, dangling two feet above the shallow river as the new sun glints off the water has me scared. The beauty. The inevitability. I wish my mother and father were home. But the sound of their woozy key in the door is still hours away.

I stagger to the scale. Two, almost three, pounds over. More cals: push-ups, sit-ups, running in place, squat-thrusts, up-downs, leg-lifts. Until I'm drifting off. You lose weight when you sleep. If I'm still heavy in the morning, I'll chop off my toes. Let the house get darker. Like blindness. Some goddam blind kid waiting in the black for me, standing on the Owl Creek Bridge.

The sound of my mother's exclamation woke me and, before I even realized that I had been dreaming, I felt the pain above my eyebrow, then the light from my parents' bedside lamp through my blindfold.

"Travis, get up. Fritzy cut himself."

"What?" answered my father sleepily.

"Sleepwalking again. He ran into something."

By then I felt something running down my cheek, catching in the rag binding my eyes, a scarlet tint through which lamplight flickered; then my dad holding onto me, lifting the blindfold off my head, dabbing it gently around the cut.

To ward the blood out of the socket, I kept my cut eye shut, squinting with the other until it focused on a woman sitting at the edge of the bed, a plain white sheet fanned across her lap, her breasts surprisingly small and white, peering up at me with tears in her eyes. No lipstick. No jewelry. Hair soft in the light. She pulled the sheet up under her arms and held them out to me.

"Get some ice, Travis."

My dad laid me in my mother's lap and she wrapped her arms around me. I didn't care if she held me like this. I didn't care that hating her worked its way around to love and back again, turning in circles like a clock. She wasn't clearly my mother, the woman with the soft small breasts holding me, sadly kissing me, as my dad held an ice pack over the cut and they talked to each other as if I weren't there.

"Look how skinny he is, Travis."

"It's okay, Rita."

"He looks like a skeleton. I want him to quit this team. Walking around with a blindfold, starving himself."

"I think it's fine, Rita."

"It's not fine. What if he needs a psychiatrist?"

"Maybe we can get a group rate."

"Travis, I'm worried. Look at him."

My mother started crying, something she never did unless she was furious. But this wasn't that wit's end murderous frustrating cry, but something that I had never heard. Something much deeper and practiced that made me raise my hand from where it rested in her lap and touch her face, wet as if she'd lifted it to the rain. I would have cried too had I been able, had it been worthwhile—a cup: half a pound of sorrow—but, too fatigued, too wrung out for crying, I merely smiled, one of those neurasthenic child-martyr smiles vouchsafed in stained glass. I slipped off the bed and limped to the scales: eighty-six pounds.

My diet never varied. Never. For breakfast I ate a piece of Hollywood bread toasted, no butter, no margarine; half a grapefruit; and a glass of orange juice. No lunch: maybe an orange or two. For supper, every blessed night, I would eat a steak my father had broiled rare before leaving for work and left wrapped in aluminum foil in the oven, a salad he left in the refrigerator, and a glass of skim milk. If I took in water, I swished it around my mouth and spit it out. No other food under any circumstances. Ever.

The day of a match, I always ate breakfast at school. I'd rise earlier than usual. My parents, behind their closed bedroom door, would be into their third or so hour of sleep, their stale restaurant garb scattered about downstairs, glasses with boozy ice still melting at their places at the kitchen table along with a nest of cigarette butts lolling in the ashtray. I'd make two thin sandwiches for lunch: a chipped ham and Swiss cheese and a peanut butter and jelly, both on Hollywood.

I'd heft up my books, gym bag, and lunch and pace three blocks to the bus island at Penn and Highland to wait in the wind and snow with the other strangers for the City 73. Sometimes I got a seat, but more often I dangled from a ceiling strap, slung with my bags, juking with each spasm of stop-start, the icy gale knifing through the center door, chilling me as I sweated in my coat and tie under a wool toggle coat in the overheated box, until dropped off in front of Saint Sebastian's.

My first stop was room 013, the wrestling room, to strip naked and weigh, assure myself that I'd be able to eat. Then to the cafeteria, half-illuminated and empty except for a few kids dozing until the bell. From the machines I'd buy an eight-ounce carton of skim milk and a package of Suzy-Qs: two slabs of chocolate cake sandwiching a layer of snow-white sugary cream. I lingered over my pre-match breakfast like it was a sacrament, believing it to have great restorative powers: each cloying bite, a pittance of milk, leaving it in my mouth until it dissolved. Happy, if that's what ten minutes of food stupor can be called, but not carefree. How quickly could I rid my body of what I had eaten? On match days I snuck into 013 five or six times to weigh. I was terrified that at weigh-in, when I stepped naked on the official scale with everyone looking on, and the ref dragged the heavy stylus across the steel bar imprinted with numbers, that it would not silently balance, but clang with my failure.

For lunch I ate one or two sandwiches, depending on my weight, and another carton of skim milk. Over the day, I'd feel strength returning to me, little by little, but also a tingle, near numbness, that started in my groin and spread throughout my body until come match time I was so nervous, so shaky, I could barely feel my extremities.

After weigh-ins—I always made weight, but God help one of Brother's wrestlers who didn't—I would eat one more time: three Nestlé chocolate bars, a tiny box of raisins, and water. Enough to give me a jolt, but not enough to make me sluggish or sick once I hit the mat. I didn't need help getting sick. I was nervous, yes, but beyond nerves lurked a kind of fear that cinched up inside me like a black sack: vertigo, the shakes, icy sweats, jagged breathing, our little gym folding up on me. I learned to not look at my opponents, the other 88s, at weigh-ins: their skanky naked bodies, mainly lowerclassmen, like me, hairless, starved, their various scars, gray button penises and testicles shivering between girly legs in the too-cold or too-hot locker room's flickering inflorescence, a pack of inmates waiting to be fumigated.

Worse were the upperclassmen 88s, tiny grown men, embittered, carnie side-shows: veiny muscles, cruel little mustaches, chest hair, and wiry black nests of exaggerated genitals. They sneered like they'd eat me. Their spit was poisonous. I kept my eyes on the tile until I was summoned by the ref to weigh; then, after dismounting the scale, scurry off, slip into sweats, and suck on chocolate until time to suit up. I didn't want to know a thing about any of them. One glance into their eyes, especially, and I was finished. I wouldn't even watch my opponent during warm-ups, nor as we stood across the mat from each other getting last-minute instructions from our coaches. Not until we met in the middle of the mat to shake hands. And not really even then. By then I could smell him, but it was too late to run.

I wrestled a boy once in my very first scrimmage who, after shaking hands in the middle of the mat, reached down to his hip and detached his leg, then stood there stork-like holding it in his hand. For a moment I didn't understand that the glistening beige leg was a prosthetic. I thought that somehow he had actually removed his leg, his real flesh-and-blood leg, that I was witnessing a phenomenon, perhaps not unusual in the realm of wrestling. I gaped and then it clicked. Clicked almost audibly, at least enough that it must have registered with him. Because he smirked, tossed the leg to the bench, and hopped after me. I was so aghast, I forgot what I was doing. He dropped to his lone knee and threw me over in a fireman's carry. His upper body was tungsten. He grunted bulldog-like as he rooted to the mat and bellied after me. I spent all three periods writhing on my back, trying to avoid his pin.

Another early scrimmage opponent had muscular dystrophy. Big-headed, clumsy, spastically leaping at me like a busted toy as I kept just out of his reach and wondered what to do. Between periods, Brother commanded me to wrestle or he'd throw in the towel. The white towel he kept draped on the back of his metal folding chair. He'd fling it into the middle of the mat if someone dogged it. He didn't mind you getting your ass kicked, but you better not give up. He jammed a thick finger into my chest. "You better learn to beat the halt and the lame, son. What are you going to do when a whole wrestler gets his hands on you? If the devil showed up at your door with his arm in a sling and an alms cup would you invite him in? You get out there and beat that boy, Sweeney, or you're walking home." We were clear out in Westmoreland County, and I knew he wasn't kidding. I took the kid on points, feinted to his bad side and double-heeled him every time he stumped in for a take-down, let him gag for breath as I held him face down on the mat with a forearm and watched the last few seconds melt off the clock.

By the time the actual season got underway, I hated wrestling, but I found myself good at it. All my life, in a neighborhood where playing ball was the only validation for boys, I had never been good at any sport. I wasn't a speedy runner; balls clattered from my hands. I discovered, however, that I possessed a kind of plodding endurance, perhaps the gift to suffer indefinitely, a shortcut through purgatory. I was good not because I was brave or skilled, but because I was so terrified of losing. Like my soul would be spirited away on the spiked banner of Mephistopheles. There for everyone to see, though I needn't have worried. No one ever showed up to watch wrestling matches.

So traumatized at the thought of being beaten, I was thankful my parents worked every evening, making it impossible for them to attend a match. My dad commiserated about this. He wanted to come and root for me; he thought it was a noble thing that I was sticking my neck out. He'd have never done it, he confessed. That's for damn sure, my mother would say. She asked only if I won or lost and, regardless of my answer, she didn't respond. She figured it was like TV: two chooches in Speedos running the ropes, punching and flopping on top of each other, a kind of sanctioned street fight. She wanted me to win. More than I wanted to win. It seemed she was holding something against me, that at times she mistook me for my dad and laid into me with the same belittling jabs. *Look at you. Like a dead cat. Girls weigh eighty-eight pounds. Not boys. What kind of fixation is this? A mental illness is what it is.* I'd be sitting there with a comic book chewing Juicy Fruit and spitting in a jar. Another Sunday, church bells at Saints Peter and Paul chiming above our snow-covered roof. The Green Goblin had just unmasked Spiderman, subdued him with an "asphyxiation grenade," and trussed him in coils of steel alloy. Reduced merely to Peter Parker, Spidey gaped in astonishment as the Goblin prepared to finish him off. In another panel, puckered Aunt May Parker muttered: "Poor Peter . . . He's a frail young man—and the city can be so cold—so merciless." *I'm going to make an appointment with a psychiatrist. Is that what I should do? Or maybe I'm the one who should check into Mayview?* Shut up, I'd think. Just shut the fuck up and let me read. *Look at me when I talk to you.*

I told her that, yes, checking into Mayview would be a good idea. My dad laughed. She snatched the comic book out of my hand, ripped it in half, and wheeled out of the room. She didn't speak to us for week.

One Tuesday night we were wrestling Immaculate Conception. Third match of the year. My record was 2-0. I stood in front of our bench, pulling up my knee pads, stretching, waiting for Brother to pace over and crack my back. Trying to keep down the rusty fear ascending my esophagus, careful to not look toward IC's bench, I let my eyes rove around the gym. Nobody much. A few parents, a few kids from school. A handful of brothers in their long severe black habits. On the balcony, above the entrance to the gym, stood a statue of Saint Sebastian, one of the early martyrs, the school's namesake, and, according to Brother, the patron saint of wrestling.

I was fascinated with Saint Sebastian, or, actually, the way he was typically portrayed in iconography: just a breechclout barely covering his crotch, bound to a tree, a dozen arrows protruding from his milky skin, their entries marked with dollops of blood. Young and muscular, a wooly head of brown hair, wholly undaunted, nearly pleased, it seemed, that he is being murdered so thoroughly, so beautifully.

I liked looking at Sebastian, but also had the feeling that I should turn away, not risk studying him too long. His agony seemed so private, yet eroticized as well: that breechclout, those arrows thrusting out of his thighs and torso as he contemplated the last seconds of his life on earth. He had been on display up there, dying, since the school was dedicated in 1927. One of his eyebrows was chipped. There was a crack in his chin. Various fissures veined his body. He seemed to be graying as the brown paint coloring his long hair flecked off, leaving the sallow plaster. Several of the metal arrows were bent. We draped towels off them, and suit coats during the gym dances. Often he wore a necktie. It had become an unconscious ritual for me to gaze up at him after stepping to the middle of the mat to shake the hand of the other 88. He never looked back at me, just went on with his dying. I'd wonder where his faith had been at that last interminable moment. Then I'd feel the hand of the other boy in mine, rake his face once like I was peering into a mirror, and wait for the ref's command to wrestle.

I figured the IC kid for a piker. Bangs like Pugsley's on *The Addams Family*, trunks pulled up nearly to his chest, a doughy roundish body. Like he was ten years old and wanted to make friends. But you can never tell. Most of the 88s, mostly freshmen, myself included, looked like babies, almost feminine, kids who just hadn't hit their growth yet. Voices hadn't even changed. But that girlishness and baby fat often concealed a practiced viciousness (something I lacked, but supplemented with fear), so I never took chances. I sparred a bit, checking this kid out. But there was no edge to him at all. He ambled flat-footed about the mat, waiting for me to do something. We locked up and accidentally cracked heads. Stars slowly pinwheeled in front of me. Then terrible pain: like an icy crowbar had been rammed through my skull, just behind my eyes.

I backed off, glanced up at Saint Sebastian. He was trying like mad to get his hands loose. Pugsley moved in on me, then suddenly shape-shifted into a coiling upperclassman with two days' growth of razor stubble and a hunger he had nursed for four years just so he could break his fast on my carcass. Sebastian lifted his head off his shoulder and returned my glance. I don't think anybody else caught it. Then he smiled, sadly, knowingly, like: *Fritzy, my man, you are in for a first-class ass-kicking.*

My head detached itself and sailed up to the gym rafters. My abandoned body surrendered its ballast and floated. I had gone insane or died. Sebastian was smiling, the transformed Pugsley processing toward me like Jack the Ripper. Then, through the doors, under the balcony, walked Rita Sweeney. My mother. As she crossed the threshold into the gym, she flicked the cigarette she had been smoking. The wind dragged it across the parking lot, specks of fire spitting over the macadam, and behind, in the distance, just before the door clanged shut, the lights in the uppermost stories of Pitt's Cathedral of Learning shimmered.

I had to be dreaming. Or the shakes and big bang on the head. I closed my eyes, opened them again. She was still there, when she was supposed to be at her job hostessing at the Suicide King, a bar just up the street. Shit, it was a strip joint and I knew it. I told people she worked at a restaurant. She wasn't even speaking to me, or my father. She wore a short leopard dress, black high-heeled boots to her knees, and a black brushed velour blazer with huge triangular lapels. Her bleached hair was pulled back off her face and behind her ears, and down her back looped a hank of fake hair two shades whiter than the dye-job. The usual face get-up: heavy turquoise eye shadow, inky liner and mascara sutured across her eyes, waxy, nearly black lipstick. Like it had all been decoupaged on, then shellacked. Gleaming in the gym lights. Tripping under the hoop on those skinny stacked heels—*trop trop trop*—across the boards, every bit of her vibrating to the top row of bleachers. I turned my head and caught her eye. She whipped out a cigarette, and I worried that she'd light up right there, but she simply clutched it between her two fingers and stared at me.

One brazen creature, my mom. Though horrified at her every molecule, let alone her presenting herself decked out like this at Saint Sebastian's, when I had so clearly made plain that neither she nor my dad were to attend my matches, I couldn't help but admire her. She was kind of beautiful, in the same grotesque way Sebastian was beautiful. She had her share of arrows sticking out of her. In English we were reading *Oedipus Rex.* I wasn't in love with my mother and I sure as hell didn't want to bump off my dad and marry her, or any woman like her. But, in that instant, I saw why my dad couldn't turn her loose, why he put up with all her crazy shit.

"Let's go, Sweeney," Brother yelled from the bench. "Quit dancing."

The IC kid, restored to a little boy again, looked at me as if I had hurt his feelings. I drove into him with a leg-drag and took him down, scored a quick two and rode him. He had the inertia of a big dead fish. Hunkered face down on the mat, my left forearm mashing his mouth into the stiff blue rubber, he moaned softly as I shot a half nelson with my right and attempted to jack him over. He stiffened. Like a stubborn toddler you can't get in his high chair. I levered with that half, his shoulder blades nearly touching each other—he had to have been in serious pain—so that he knew that if he didn't want a shoulder that could rotate like a ball turret, he'd better lie down on his back and take it from there.

But I couldn't pin him, couldn't get that ref, lying on his striped chest, running his palm between the mat and the kid's back to see if there was space. I couldn't get that ref to slap the mat; my mother, on her feet, screaming, "C'mon, Fritzy. Kill him. Kill him, Fritzy." Screaming, jockeying with her whole body, like when she got really pissed off over a conversation she had just had with her mother, my grandmother, who we never saw because there was bad blood they'd been trying to sort out for years, part of which had something to do with my dad. It wasn't any of my business. It had started before I was born. Or pissed at my dad because he always had his nose in the newspaper, because for a living—a grown man, pig-shit Irish from Pierce Street—he was content to wear a yes-man monkey suit and kiss people's asses for tips at the Park Schenley. Pissed because, like him, I had no ambition and would amount to nothing. Cut us off like gangrene. Up there standing on the top of the bleachers in that leopard outfit, the bleached hair, black roots stitched along the part, going on and on: "Cream him, Fritzy." Attracting attention, and I'm lying on top of this kid, his eyes closed, suffering me, waiting for the clock to buzz, like I'm some kind of operation he must endure, sweat bealing out of him all over both of us and puddling the mat.

But I could not pin him and get out of there, and my mother rioting. All three periods, six minutes in all, each red second exploding on the wall clock, and he wouldn't give up. I kicked the shit out of him: take-down, predicament, near-pin; cradling him the entire last period, furious that he refused to give it up, trying God help me to break his neck just to be done with it and placate Rita Sweeney with his murder. Rip his head off and throw it at her. He suffered every bit of it like contentment: *Gimme another arrow.* All I was left with after a 15-0 decision was my arm hoisted by the referee and my shame, drenched in that other boy's sweat.

Brother looked at me as I came off the mat, then looked away. Before I even collapsed next to the mat to blow into the bucket, my mother left, same swagger as if an entourage were trailing her. And Sebastian returned to his death throes. I'd never know, nor would my dad, what it was that would make her happy. She was bad news, but neither of us knew how to stop loving her.

Two days before the match with the Blind, I wrestled in practice a kid named Antonucci, a junior who outweighed me by fifteen pounds. He was a kid I didn't like, and though I was a better wrestler, he bullied me with his extra heft. He smelled like hell and had scabby sideburns and a cauliflower ear that bloomed like a loose brain off the side of his head. About fifty splinters of dirty black hair spiked out of his upper lip. I felt them against my cheek as he rode me, grinding my blindfolded face into the mat, whispering obscenities into my ear. Winded, I struggled to get to my knees and throw a move. But he was too heavy and I couldn't budge. Then he licked the back of my neck with his feline tongue and whispered, "Your mother greases elevator chains. And I greased her last night."

I relaxed and felt him mortised atop me. Then I buckled up from the mat with all I had and switched him, shot a half and spilled him over on his back for the pin. He grabbed my crotch and squeezed until I had no choice but to let go. I bolted up. Antonucci threw me into the wall. Something cracked the bridge of my nose. An electric current of red streaked across my blindfold, then it was as if a fire had been set behind my eyes and hot cable pulled through my nose. Still blindfolded, I went after Antonucci. I heard him laughing. Blood filled my mouth. I heard Brother's whistle, and the sound of jostling bodies came to an abrupt halt.

"Take off the blindfolds," Brother barked; then, "Come up here, Antonucci."

Brother went to the first aid box and brought out a pair of pliers. "In two days," he said, "we wrestle the Blind, and you may think, because they can't see you, that your appearance doesn't matter; but it does. In fact it matters more because they're blind. You're going to look your absolute best, not just because you're Saint Sebastian's, which is plenty, but most important, out of respect for their affliction, for the fact that they can't see you. Understand?"

The team murmured in unison, "Yes, sir."

Brother glanced at me a few times as he spoke. I held the blindfold to my nose. It bled, but not terribly. I felt my nose filling my face, crowding my eyes, a spreading gleam of pain drilling the roof of my mouth. I watched Antonucci, standing next to Brother at the front of 013, an anxious look on his face.

"White shirts, coats, and ties in here two hours before the match, polished shoes and clean shaves," Brother commanded.

Then Brother, holding the pliers, turned to Antonucci. "You know what a clean shave looks like, Antonucci?"

"Yes, Brother."

"Good, but just in case, step over here, and I'll get you started."

Antonucci just looked at Brother.

"Get over here, boy."

Antonucci minced two steps closer. Brother snared him by his shirtfront and yanked him the rest of the way. "If you move," he threatened, then began yanking out the hairs on Antonucci's lip one by one with the pliers. Antonucci stood it silently and without flinching, his eyes melting more with each extraction, until his raw red hairless lip glowed and his eyes had closed entirely.

"Blindfolds on. Hit it for push-ups, then out in the hall for sprints," Brother boomed. "Back to the tyranny of darkness, gentlemen."

After practice I was headed to the locker room when Brother shouted, "Fall out, Sweeney. Take off the blindfold."

I walked over to him where he stood in the hall, idly forearming the wall and humming the *Ave Maria.* He wore, as always, his black, floor-length habit, at the very bottom of which peaked a pair of cuffed khakis and black coaching shoes with heavy slant tread.

"Yes, Brother?"

"C'mere."

He ushered me into the first floor lavatory and pointed to the long wall mirror above the urinals. I stood there, a small, inconsequential body afloat in sweat and grime and swallowed in stretched clothes too large for me. My head was tiny, marble white except for the cap of black hair and heavy eyebrows. My eyes looked white. I had no mouth. In the center of my blank face bloomed a wild rose, its outer petals peeled back to reveal its bloody heart. My nose, two clicks to the left, rested nearly beneath my eye. At the bridge was a horizontal red slash.

"It's broken," I pronounced.

"Yep."

I stared a moment longer at this face, wholly divorced, it felt, from the *who,* even the *what,* I thought of as myself, as if I might rub it from existence with a swipe at the glasss, or leave this image smudged to the mirror and find another, wander mirror to mirror for the rest of my life until I discovered my proper face.

Brother stood behind me, his long, bespectacled, scholarly face sitting on top of mine in the mirror. "You want to go to the hospital?" he asked. "Or you want me to fix it? It's a clean break."

It was guts Brother loved. He had rooted Japs out of tunnels in Saipan in World War II, and still kept his hair in a Parris Island buzz cut. *Semper fi*, he'd bark during practice and pep talks. Two tours in Korea. He had played football in the Corps, then pro in Canada for the Montreal Alouettes, going both ways for an entire season with a double hernia, with *nothing for a jock but a peanut shell and a rubber band*, as he liked to say, and finally a year in the NFL with the Redskins.

I looked at that exaggerated smear reflecting back at me under Brother's chin. His eyes were so lethally blue that they beamed right through the lenses of his glasses and careened back off the mirror at me.

"You fix it, Brother."

He covered my face with his hand, and I felt my nose slide back into place. Tears rolled out of my eyes. The left one beginning to discolor. Brother yanked a roll of white adhesive tape out of his pocket, ripped off a length with his teeth, and fixed it across my nose.

"You see this," he said, turning his profile to me. His nose looked like the head of a ball-peen hammer. He held up an open hand. "Five times busted."

I looked around the locker room for Antonucci, but he'd already cleared out. A few guys were still in the shower. DeRiso, hairy as a man of forty, stood in there with Dennis Devet, his good pal—the two co-captains. Devet, another senior, was the best wrestler on the team, perennial diocesan champ, All-Catholic, undefeated, two-time defending state champ on his way to Dartmouth—full boat—on a bead for his third state title in the 95-pound class. He weighed only seven pounds more than me, an old man crammed into a little boy's pensive body: all bailing wire and gravel, skin wrung so tightly it looked tattooed to his frame, veins and capillaries, red and blue, rushing along its ashen hairless surface like traffic, his face a skull, tangled brown curls nesting on his crown, the rest of his head bristle. He was double-jointed and, in matches, would devil his opponents by turning himself nearly inside out, slithering out of their grasp like a snake. On the mat he was an executioner, a wrestler who trained every finger to seduce his opponent, who dealt pain, and suffered it with dogged acceptance. Next to DeRiso, plump and shaggy, Devet looked like one of the Jewish bodies scraped into ditches by Nazi bulldozers in *Night and Fog*, a movie Brother made us watch in Christian Doctrine. After matches, Devet and DeRiso drove in Devet's pink LeMans down Two Mile Run into Hazlewood to drink beer and cherry vodka.

Unconsciously soaping and resoaping, I slumped into a pink fiberglass chair someone had left under a fizzing showerhead, letting the spray, gradually growing tepid, play over me, every few seconds spitting quids of blood onto the tile floor. DeRiso was spouting about the match. He didn't see how you could lose to a blind kid. It defied logic. After all, they can't see. Like a blind army versus an army with sight. Who's going to win? Who you going to bet on? Brother was just doing a psyche job on us, building up the blind team because he felt sorry for them, and didn't want us to have a moment's peace about it. How he had massacred us in practice all week, the blindfolds, the whole bit, because he wanted us to do penance for being blessed with sight. Everything was religion with Brother: parables, lessons, the Marine version of the Beatitudes.

"Let's be rational," DeRiso insisted. "You go out, you jack 'em up, slam 'em down and pin 'em. Boom. Nothing malicious. Just get it over with. They're blind. They can't see. Child's play."

DeRiso's argument made perfect sense to me. Yes, we had to maintain contact at all times, but it would be easy enough, it seemed, after the initial lock-up, to swipe a leg, fireman's carry, a half dozen moves, to topple him, then move directly in for the pin. Nevertheless, Brother had me spooked. I believed in him so completely that his warnings about the prowess of the blind wrestlers had taken root. I feared my blind opponent precisely because of his sightlessness, as if it were a power that privileged, rather than limited, him. I envisioned him scrabbling to his feet after pinning me, his arms raised in victory. Finally, like in a nightmare, I'd be invisible, nonexistent. I could not determine if there were more shame in beating a blind boy or losing to one.

"How's the nose, Sweeney?" DeRiso asked.

"Broken."

"You were never going to win an Academy Award with that mug anyhow."

"Nah."

"Listen. I got a good news/bad news joke for you. You want to hear it?"

"Go ahead."

"Okay. This lady just had a baby. So the doctor comes in and says, 'I have some good news, and some bad news. Whatta you want to hear first?' So the lady says, 'Gimme the good news,' and the doctor says, 'You just gave birth to a ten-pound eyeball.' The lady is, of course, understandably upset at this startling news. 'What could be worse?' she asks, and the doctor says, 'It's blind.'"

When I smiled, my nose started bleeding.

"Here's another one," DeRiso smirked. "How did Helen Keller's parents punish her?" Everyone was still laughing at the eyeball joke, and when no one answered, DeRiso said, "Rearrange the furniture."

"Now ponder this," he continued. "If God is love, and love is blind, is Ray Charles God?"

Devet, who hadn't so much as looked at me, finally spoke up: "That's as far as I'll go with this discussion, DeRiso. I don't believe in making fun, not that I want you to get the impression that I give a shit whether these people can see or not, but discussing them at all gets into the realm of superstition. Walking onto the mat with a blind kid is just another big-time way to fail. One second of inattention, of hesitation, and you're on your back."

"You, maybe; but there's not a blind boy on this planet who can kick my ass."

"Pride goeth before a fall, my man," Devet snapped.

Oedipus's tragic flaw was pride. He thought he could outfox the gods. He jabbed his eyes out with Jocasta's gold brooches. His mom was his wife. He killed his dad. His daughters were his sisters. The cover of our book showed a bearded guy with a crown, smears of bright dripping scarlet where his eyes had been. His lips were parted, his mouth a black hole. The whole thing was outlandish, but he and his family could have been hiding out in any house in my neighborhood.

The only blind guy I knew was Mooch, a kind of self-styled neighborhood shaman who supposedly could see the future. Every day he slumped in a chair outside Nardini's on Hoeveler Street with a tin cup at his feet and predicted the outcome of football and baseball games. The kicker was he had a blind dog too. But I always crossed the street when I reached his block. The last thing I would have risked was knowing my future. If I knew it, it would probably come true. Like Oedipus's. *Not* knowing it would allow me to change it.

And there were the guys with spooky black glasses who stood on Penn Avenue peddling pencils for change, and the people my mother bought brooms and lightbulbs from when they called on the phone. But that was the extent of my experience with the blind. Brother Benedict, our English teacher, told us that we should keep in mind that Oedipus's blindness was also a metaphor. It wasn't the metaphor that scared me, but the blood gushing out of Oedipus's mutilated eyes every time he stuck them. Wrestling a metaphor wouldn't have worried me at all.

Before he left the shower, Devet dropped right there and blew off fifty fingertip push-ups. A few minutes later, as the hot water went gradually cold, I heard the scale squealing as he bartered with it. More than once, I'd seen him, in a last-ditch attempt to make weight on the way to a match, run up and down the bus aisle in a rubber sweat suit. Then he was gone, and DeRiso too, then all of them, frozen air fluting through the door leading out to the quadrangle, in the middle of which the Blessed Mother statue huddled in the cold. I sat there in the icy shower until I could no longer stand it.

Brother didn't traffic much in metaphors either. He told us in Religion that if he thought the host was just a symbol, he'd spit it out. Symbols, he said, were for doggers, breakers without the will. He believed with all his heart—stabbing me in the chest with his long finger as he talked—that that host, Holy Communion, was the unequivocal, undoctored, nonmetaphorical body and blood of our savior Jesus Christ. Period. He once discovered me passed out on a bench in the locker room. I'd snuck up there during lunch to boil away a pound or two in the whirlpool. When I climbed out of the scalding stainless steel tank, I must have fainted. I came to with Brother waving a jug of ammonia under my nose. The second I was back in the world he started in about Communion, how every day he went to Mass and received the Eucharist. I didn't understand a thing he said, at least not that day, lying scorched and naked on that gray wooden bench. Brother liked talking about the illusion of our bodies. He insisted there was something about ourselves we didn't know, something that in 013 he could extort with a look and forearm shiver. Then he'd tell you that this mystery was God, not him, not you. God. Then shake you down for the change in your pockets to ship off to the missions.

The Western Pennsylvania School for the Blind was on Bellefield Street, not even half a mile from Saint Sebastian's. Built in 1894 on land donated by the Schenley family, it was four massive stories of dingy red brick, surrounded by lawns and hedges and enormous black trees. The grounds teemed with people, many of them blindfolded, gripping canes, and guided by sighted persons. They were being prepared, I assumed, for their inevitable blindness. Others with canes and dark glasses walked confidently along the gravel paths, carrying books. Brother told us that the school trained these children to enter the world as piano tuners, switchboard operators, typists, even plumbers. He told us we were a bunch of prima donnas, that we better not feel sorry for the blind team; they'd be coming after us.

Weaving our way silently through them, and entering the building through its gothic concrete arches, we were led down a long corridor. On its walls were mounted framed, autographed photographs of famous personalities like the Lone Ranger, Phyllis Diller, and even Eleanor Roosevelt surrounded by beaming little blind children. We took a side door and dropped down an ill-lit staircase, and were suddenly in the dim, dingy locker room—Brother reciting the Litany of the Most Precious Blood of Jesus, followed by Psalm 69 (*Hear me, O Lord; for Thy loving kindness is good; turn unto me according to the multitude of Thy tender mercies*), during the entire journey.

As we undressed, the ref came in to explain that we had to maintain contact to afford our opponents access to us through, in his exact words, *uninterrupted touch.* Brother kicked a roll of tape around the locker room, singing in Latin the *Tantum Ergo*, pausing every minute or so to bark at us, "Hurry up."

The scale stood in a small room adjacent to the swimming pool. As we waited to weigh in, we watched blind children in orange life vests flail along in the water while lifeguards, stationed at either end of the pool, blew unceasingly in their whistles.

The blind team, naked like us, herded in to weigh behind their coach, a tall, apologetic fat guy in a coat and tie who quickly shook hands with Brother and guided each of his wrestlers up to the scale. I had assured myself dozens of times that I would not lay eyes on my opponent until we shook hands before the match, but I ended up watching every one of them, guided by their sweating coach, trip onto the scales, bump into things, fumble through every step of the weigh-in.

Their 88, a black kid who never stopped grinning, had the exaggerated pecs and biceps from pushing a barbell, but still seemed starved. He looked eight years old, but his hair was spotted with gray and he wore a goatee. His eyes were one-color-white: when he rolled them, when he looked straight ahead, when he glanced down at the numbers he could not see—dead-on weight—or at the coach who pointed him back toward the locker room to get dressed. And he had an erection, uncircumcised, ashen, gnarled.

Stripped literally of every pretense, I detested the public nudity, the queued wait until it was my turn to mount the scale and suck in my breath, palms down so the ref could inspect my fingernails and pronounce exactly what I amounted to: eight ounces shy of eighty-eight pounds. Not much.

When we emerged from the locker room and ran to the middle of the mat for warm-up, we were met with pandemonium. The gym was rickety and shrouded in gauzy light. High-tiered bleachers, rafters to floor, overflowed with people, screaming and gesticulating. When a garbled electrical voice announced us, the spectators began stamping their feet. The gym quaked. Brother yelled at us from the bench, but we couldn't hear a thing.

As we retired to the bench, the loudspeakers screeched again and the blind team was led to the mat. The gym went berserk. Spectators hung dangerously from the uppermost tiers, clapping, whistling. The blind wrestlers, in ill-fitting, mismatched uniforms, stumbled through their warm-up. As soon as they left the mat, a quartet of cheerleaders, dressed also in tattered uniforms, carrying pompons, shuffled to the mat and erupted into a series of confused spastic cheers. Pretty girls, yet each transmogrified: dark glasses, a marble eye lolling in too deep a socket, barrettes askew, lipstick off the mark. One of them dropped a pompon. Though it was nearly touching her shoe tops, she made a dozen passes for it before she located it, smiling the while, as the other girls, oblivious, went on without her.

Brother had me on my feet. He hoisted me in a reverse bear hug and I heard my spine click as he squeezed. From his embrace I watched my opponent step to the middle of the mat, same grin, his head swiveling and cocked as if waiting for me to come to him and whisper in his ear. Brother's heart pushed against my back. "Deign, O God, to rescue me," he said. "O Lord, make haste to help me." Then: "Get out there, Sweeney," and pushed me onto the mat.

We shook hands, and the ref locked us up: one of my hands behind his neck, another on the wrist on the hand he placed behind my neck; his other hand on my wrist. Then the ref chopped down his hand and barked, "Wrestle."

There were days when my father told me I was too religious, that it was all bullshit, that when you died there was a round of *Amens*, a pittance of silence, and then the party went on without you. He hadn't told me this out of spite or cruelty, but cynicism, his way of telling me to wring all I could from the moment. Maybe wrestling, starving myself in particular, was my way of killing myself without taking the bridge, like freezing to death or drowning. Simply going to sleep. Goddam, it was nothing but fear. Blind fear. And I was locked up with it. Suddenly I wished my crazy, brazen mother, surrounded by that sea of sightless lunatics, was in the stands, shrieking above their ungodly clamor for me to kill this kid, blind or not, swab the mat with him, lay waste to him and anything that got in my way. She'd never give up. That was for sure. Not Rita Sweeney. Once revved up, she'd scrape her own skin off with an emery board, layer by layer, out of sheer spite for herself.

But it was Brother shouting. For me to quit dancing, for me to wrestle, that he was about to throw in the towel. I heard in his voice accusation, the indictment of my spirit. I was being backed off the mat by my opponent. He smelled like an old man. His big strong hands holding my cheek against his. I remembered to open my eyes. He was smiling. Starchy eyes. His lips an inch from mine like he wanted to kiss me. When I jerked back, he held on, walloping his face against mine, then suddenly peeling off, both hands for some reason over his ears, still smiling, but kettling out a thin whistling hiss. The ref called time, but it was me he was looking at, my singlet covered in blood. My busted nose.

We each went to our benches. I lay down on the mat, Brother crouched over me.

"What the hell's the matter with you, Sweeney?"

I tried to answer, but my mouth swam in blood. I tilted my head and it rolled out onto the mat.

"You wanna wrestle, boy?"

I nodded.

He pulled a tampon out of his habit and jammed it up the bleeding nostril. I felt it disappear into my brain. For an instant, there was a red downpour just behind my eyeballs, and the pain lifted me off the mat.

"Go to work, Sweeney," Brother said softly.

The ref locked us up again. I swallowed a glass of blood and slid down the black kid's body, looped around and double-heeled him to the mat. I rode him for maybe twenty seconds, getting a blow, gulping down blood, flooded with nausea. Beneath me, he seemed helpless and content, as I tied him up with double chicken wings and then gaffed him over on his back. He bucked, but in the end he wasn't very strong at all and I imagined him admiring the ceiling lights through his cottony eyes as the ref banged the mat.

The fans, unaware of what had happened, rocked jubilantly, loudspeakers yammering in the rafters. My opponent sprang to his feet and, as if the match had never ended, reached out and snagged me by the back of my uniform. I turned and he tumbled on me. Instinctively, I threw him to the mat, fell on him to pin him again, when the ref and both coaches, hurrying from their benches, broke us up. The black boy smiled and waved his hand at me. I took it and we shook. The ref lifted my arm in victory. I staggered to our bench with Brother's help. He yanked out the tampon, spooling blood, and I vomited in the bucket.

Devet stepped out there next. Sheer starving wired intensity. Manic hair. Voodoo superstition on top of die-hard Vatican Catholicism. On the mat, Devet was the inquisition, and he didn't like what he was seeing. His kid shimmered with contemplative defiance. Actually had eyes: iris, pupil, cornea, lens. Even a color: bright pine green. That reckoned something, not sight in any ocular sense, but something only a blind man can see: oracular, Tiresias, playing possum, hobbling up to the palace gates. Like my kid, Devet's opponent seemed old too. A grown man, but tiny. Ninety-five pounds. Yet somehow large nevertheless.

A genius on his feet, Devet had not been taken down once in the past couple of seasons. He had this very odd manner. Moving in like a snake charmer, tilted to starboard, wiggling his long spidery fingers in and out, kind of grooving, almost effeminate. All the freshmen imitated him. The forced lock-up with the blind 95, however, instantly threw him. Devet was bone-gaunt, but had that tensile, cockstrong strength of the upperclassmen who wrestled the puny weights. Like they had internal generators that would kick in when they needed an extra boost. Some of us underclassmen had yet to sprout pubic hair. But the blind kid had short, veiny blue arms with biceps that looked like snakes choking on baseballs. He muscled Devet over and had him on his back inside twenty seconds. But not for long. Devet rolled to his stomach, turned a double-jointed Houdini, and threw a whizzer that would have taken the kid's arm off if he hadn't let go.

The ref locked them up again, and the kid took Devet down again. Devet sat out, never lost contact, and executed an arm duck-under called a Syracuse. Thorough sleight-of-hand. If it happens to you, you think you're wrestling two people. Your guy is in front of you, and then he's behind you, like he slipped into this invisible hole and disappeared for two seconds. The blind kid was mystified. His eyes glowed, and the veins in his shaved head swelled. He started to stand up, but Devet grabbed an ankle and drove him face first into the mat, then mashed his cheek into the rubber. The kid got to his knees. Devet worked a leg behind his bent near knee, then sprawled across his back, and grabbed the far arm. The kid did exactly what he shouldn't have done, exactly what Devet wanted him to do: he pulled that arm away, and when he did, Devet ducked his head under the arm and, using the momentum of the kid's recoil, rolled him 180 onto his back in a crucifix, sometimes called a guillotine. It was a near impossible move to effect, because in the split-instant of rolling your opponent, you had to get hold of his other arm, and control his free leg with your free leg as well, so that when the spinning stopped, you had him staked out like the Lamb of God. You needed the touch and hubris of a bomb expert and Devet's double-jointedness (DeRiso called him an invertebrate). One little slip and it would be you on your back.

The green-eyed blind boy could not move, except to flutter his fingertips and bat his eyes. Like a paralytic. His hands and feet nailed down. When he tried to bridge, Devet drove his forehead into the kid's cheekbone. The kid yodeled for breath, a shriek, and then the ref blasted his hand against the mat.

Devet's was the only real match. One by one the blind wrestlers moved to the mat like zombies. Our wrestlers stalled a bit, until nudged by Brother's voice; then they belted them down and pinned them. The blind took their beatings with aplomb and obliviousness and were led back to the bench by their coach. After every few matches, the cheerleaders stumbled out to cheer. The bedlam grew. At some point, the announcer ceased his play-by-play. Even Brother, perhaps hoping that one of us might lose, for the sake of Christian piety, fell silent.

Their heavyweight—the last match—was a squat, pink, outlandishly obese kid with a scowl and no eyes at all, as if his sockets had been puttied up, and no eyebrows. Brother cracked DeRiso's back. Our bench was completely silent. Devet sat with a towel over his head. I held an ice pack to my face.

"Okay, DeRiso," Brother said above the dull roar.

"Brother," DeRiso uttered, almost pleadingly.

"I know. Let's get it over with and go home."

After locking up, DeRiso couldn't get the kid off his feet. He was deadweight, with the same center of gravity as a refrigerator. DeRiso slid him around, but couldn't do a thing. DeRiso had this trick of butting in the lock-up, ramming his giant head, which he soaked in rock salt water to thicken the skin, into the forehead or just above the eye of his opponent, every time they locked up—*bam*—bashing the other heavyweight's skull until he was wobbling. Then DeRiso would doze him over like a condemned house. One night an ambulance had to be summoned to scrape up a kid DeRiso had pounded dopy. He toppled over and rolled around the mat with both hands over his concussion.

Beginning of the second period, he gored the blind heavy, forehead to forehead. We heard it, even above all noise. Like a hardball off a block wall. Again and again. But the kid wouldn't go down. Took every hit like he was storing them, getting pinker and pinker, his entire body the color of raw salmon. The ref should've warned DeRiso, but it was like he didn't notice, or couldn't take any more himself. That *bonk* from DeRiso's head, and then another noise: something leaking, like all the air was being siphoned from the gym, all the voices being slowly bled out through the rafters, in a giant crashing suspiration as one by one the audience hushed, and the noise, that last noise, that at first I thought was coming from me, or maybe from Devet, under that towel, was coming from DeRiso. Weeping, then *bonk*, blistering that kid who didn't seemed to mind. DeRiso, in the middle of the mat, the gym now like a church when the priest elevates the host and the altar boy rings the bell three times, and you strike your breast softly in sorrow. DeRiso crying his eyes out. Brother threw in the towel. It skidded across the mat. The ref picked it up and threw it back to our bench. He whispered something in the blind heavyweight's ear, and then lifted his hand. Brother went out after DeRiso. Still crying, he collapsed when they reached the bench, and dropped his head in his hands. The PA coughed out the news of the blind heavyweight's victory, and the gym erupted again in madness.

DeRiso and Devet were headed down the Run to drink, and they asked me if I wanted to come. Couple of six packs of Schmidt's and a pint of red vodka. I didn't think it was a good idea. Not on that night. It would open up too much. Something I could wait on, something that would always be there. Everybody told DeRiso to forget about it, whatever the hell it was that happened. Brother told us that Saint Sebastian hadn't died, after all, from all those arrows the Roman archers had shot into him. Saint Irene found him and yanked every one of the arrows out, then nursed him back to health. The same guys who tried to assassinate Sebastian the first time got hold of him again, and then beat him to death. That's what Brother left us with before we climbed off the bus and headed home. A little like DeRiso's good news/bad news jokes. Then he told us he'd see us at practice the next day.

As I stood at the bus stop, waiting for the 73 to take me home, tape over my cut eye, across my broken nose and cheeks, I remembered that I still had my cane, the one I'd used all week to navigate Saint Sebastian's halls, in my book bag. I took it out. I wouldn't be needing it anymore. The bus rolled up, and, instead of throwing away the cane, I assembled it, closed my eyes, and tapped through the center doors and felt around until I found the overhead bar. The bus lurched off and I nearly fell over. Suddenly someone was at my elbow, ushering me a few steps to my left, saying, "Please, sit," gently situating me in a seat. I thanked her, by the sound of her voice a young woman. I smelled her perfume, sensed her manner as shy, erudite, late twenties, early thirties. I sat there in the dark, counting the stops, so I'd know when to get off.

At Penn and Highland, I stood and very carefully inched my way to the door, then down three steps to the curb. I felt hands easing me along, almost imperceptibly, until I was on the sidewalk. Then a rush about me as people hurried home, their shoes on the concrete, the smell of East Liberty, its very heart. Just a few yards from me, outside of East Liberty Presbyterian, there was a fountain. In its center rose Virgil Cantini's giant sculpture called *Joy of Life*: a rusted steel ring of faceless, genderless people clasped arm and arm and bent back as if to drink down the cascade of water. The grandeur of the mammoth stone church loomed over me. Richard King Mellon's church, laden with all the wealth and mystery of Pittsburgh. But I couldn't hear the fountain. It had obviously frozen.

Just a few doors up from the intersection was Anthon's, a bakery from which my father often brought home pastry. It was a white, shiny building. Like porcelain, its name scrolled in colossal royal blue across its top. On either side of the door gleamed big display windows packed with beautiful cakes and pies. I had the building memorized, inside and out. I fumbled in and slowly made my way to the glass counter behind which everything waited. Everything. At least that's what I thought. That it was all ahead of me.

When the lady asked, so kindly, if she could help me, I told her, without opening my eyes, that I wanted a dozen glazed French doughnuts, six with white icing and six chocolate. She didn't want to take my money, but I insisted. I smiled and thanked her. Back on Penn Avenue, I had the sense as I passed through the cold January evening that a way was being made for me, that people were genuflecting and bowing their heads, that they recognized in me a fearless boy, righteously burdened, who would never turn from anything.

What I had really been contemplating, I suppose I should be ashamed to say, were the doughnuts. Maybe even as I had been riding that blind boy, then watching Devet and DeRiso and the rest of them half lose their minds as one by one we stepped up to the slaughter; even as Brother rammed that tampon up my nose; even as I puked and bled and gazed at those crazy blind cheerleaders and their pack of loony blind fans. They scared the living hell out of me. But the whole time, I had been thinking of myself. Christian piety never crossed my mind. Just me—and what I'd eat after it was all over. Even if I lost. I thought of sweets.

DRIVING

When I turned sixteen, my mother insisted I learn how to operate an automobile. My father didn't drive, something my mother held against him, just as she did the fact that he did all the cooking and was addicted to the newspaper and made predictions, often dead center, about which way the world, in 1971, would lurch. A man had to drive a car. One morning she woke me at 3 A.M., after she and my father blew in from their restaurant jobs.

Illuminated by the pale light from the hall behind her, she hovered over my bed like a giant moth, arms spread cruciform in the mammoth sleeves of her short, furry leopard jacket, its spots invisible in the murk, her head voluminous, webbed in high-teased haired through which cracks of light leaked. I smelled liquor, lipstick, and hairspray, the latent rank and cloy of eight hours on her feet, followed by a string of nightcaps with my dad, and some friends, after he clocked out from waiting tables just up the street.

"Get dressed. You're learning how to drive," she commanded.

My dad stood out in the hall under the lightbulb. He had already had his say on this subject and my mother had paid no attention. I could see this by the way he undid his bow tie, then his shirt. Going down those buttons like he was playing the last sad notes on a sax. Last call. No one around to listen.

"God, Rita," he said. "Let the boy sleep."

"He's learning to drive," she pronounced. "He's not going to grow up to be helpless like you."

She closed my door behind her, then badgered me into my clothes from the other side of it while she and my dad sniped at each other. He was a gutless wonder. She was a princess. He could kiss her ass. He admired her ass, especially the way she substituted it for brains.

Dressed, I opened the door and there they were. My mother on tiptoe, those big calf muscles bulging under the sheen of her high, white patent leather zippered go-gos, arms up around my dad's neck. His hands on her hips. Shirt unbuttoned and unknotted maroon bow tie still dangling from his neck like the confessor's stole. Her leopard lay crouched on the floor. Short lacy black dress, flimsy from the waist up. Then, as if on cue, like they had rehearsed, they stopped kissing and wheeled on me.

"Get your ass in the car," my mother said, and peeled off my father. "I'm teaching you to drive."

"Rita, you couldn't teach a man on fire to jump in a swimming pool," snapped my dad.

"Then I'll die trying," she fired back at him, then winked at me.

My dad laughed, and said very plainly, "Large mistake." Then disappeared into their bedroom across the hall.

My mother sped down Negley Run Boulevard with her left arm out the window. With her right hand, she clutched the steering wheel and a lit Chesterfield. Just before we hit Washington

Boulevard, she slowed to a crawl and bumped the car over the curb into a massive grassy field at the edge of the three-storey tower used to teach firemen how to jump out of burning buildings. The tower was bathed in spotlights, and beneath it was a huge net. Firemen decked in full turnout plunged off the edge of the tower, one after another, but we couldn't see them land because of the trees in the foreground.

"Why are they doing that in the middle of the night?" I wondered out loud.

"This is when most fires start," my mother answered, then doused the headlights and switched off the ignition. "Get behind the wheel."

Our car was a used beige '61 Chevy Impala with a three-speed on the column. I didn't know what an impala was; I'm sure my mother didn't either. In the nearly full moon, the keys and the chrome in the car's interior pulsed smokily like extinguished neon. My mother demonstrated how the car started, the flick of the key in the ignition, how just the slightest pressure on the throttle was enough, often more than enough, to hurl you into the future. But as long as you had the clutch and the brake clamped hard against the floor, nothing bad could happen. She ordered me to engage the clutch; then, with her hand on mine, she guided me through the gears and their intricate relationship with speed and regret.

"Delicate" was the word she used, in the moonlight, smoking a cigarette while a stream of men flew off the tower.

Then she whispered suddenly, "Fritzy, I'm finished," and dropped her cigarette out the window. She couldn't go on a moment more. If I ever wanted to see home again, then I had to drive us there myself. Did I understand? "Things are that desperate," she said. "But everything—every little thing, Fritzy, will be fixed, put back together, I promise, if you'll drive me home. I want to go home now." Then she began to cry, an indulgence she never permitted herself.

"Mom, I don't know how to drive. I don't even have a learner's permit."

"You can drive, Fritz; I just taught you. You are going to be a man—not like your father—and take me home. Then, everything, goddammit'll be fine." Crying so hard she could barely get her breath. Gagged out the words.

I fired up the car, padded in the clutch, dropped the stick into the lower left leg of the mysterious H of the gearbox, transferred my right foot from brake to throttle, and caressed the gas. I eased up on the clutch, and clearly felt it: that in-betweenness my mother had described, the *just-before* that's always better than what's about to happen. I slid my shoe off the clutch and hit the gas. With a ravenous hiss, the Impala lifted off the earth.

LOVER

From Pittsburgh, I thumb a ride all the way out Saw Mill Run Boulevard clear into a little place called Roscoe on Route 88 leading into California, PA. Every couple miles there's the name of another town, planted in the dank roadbed, a rusted sign bolted to a stick: *Stockdale, Elco, Coal Center.* Alongside the blacktop, a train track rambles. Parallel to the track, the Monongahela River, fudge-colored and restive, coils in the last of the murky light. Its banks clump in snowed-over dead weeds and coal, dirty icicles knifing down from the decks of flat cars abandoned on the sidings.

As night slinks in, lights pop on throughout the valley. Gray. Smoky. Snow churns out of the invisible sky. No cars, so I keep walking. Then a train bangs slowly up the track. I jog next to it, grab hold of an iron rung laddering up to the roof of a boxcar and hoist myself up, my gloveless hands numb, my feet too by the time the train slices through my destination: California State College. I attempt to jump into a bank of snow, but I land funny, my paralyzed hands and feet useless, roll in the cinders and crud, banging my head and ripping my jeans. I wander around the small campus until I find McCloskey Hall, Keith's dorm.

From one of the rooms, Bachman-Turner Overdrive blares: "Welcome Home." Way too loud, especially because I'm frozen, as if I might begin to chip. I feel it: "Welcome Home." Those two-ton guitar licks in my brittle fingers and toes.

I hammer on room 251. Like I'm the cops. I hear Keith mutter something, then he opens the door, wearing an oversized purple Minnesota Vikings jersey, number 00, a red bandana snugged around his head. Ledges of wiry hair jut from beneath the bandana at right angles. A cigarette fidgeting in his mouth, he holds a cup with a spoon sticking out of it. His hands are shaking, the spoon clinking against the enamel. On his desk a candle burns—no other light—and beside it a strand of smoke, barely visible, rises from a cone of strawberry incense that makes the room smell cloyingly sweet. Like a head shop.

For a second, he looks at me like he doesn't know who I am, then says, "Fritzy," pitifully, like he might cry.

"What's the matter?" I ask.

"Number one," he announces, holding up a quaking finger, "is I'm worried to death."

"What's up?"

He paces, exaggeratedly long strides, and lights another cigarette. His girlfriend, Bonnie Guida, she might be pregnant. Her period's late. Almost two weeks. There's a framed picture of her on the block wall over his desk: in a baby blue and pink striped bikini. Long blonde hair flairs over half her face. She's looking down like an innocent teenaged Madonna at the snowy towel in her hand. Breathtakingly beautiful, achingly so. She's so perfect, guys who see the picture gasp and clap a hand over their hearts. This is Keith's girl and he guards this image of her like it's the consecrated host. But Bonnie doesn't look like that. She never did. It's like the photograph was taken with an enchanted freak camera from *The Twilight Zone.* One that metamorphoses its subjects into unattainable fantasies.

I like Bonnie. We go way back. She's a solid girl, and good to Keith, but she's faded like a lot of those East Liberty girls who don't get out in time: graduated from Peabody, got a job filing and answering the phone at Don Allen Chevrolet on Baum Boulevard, still lives at home with her parents. Keith has a retarded brother, so he's in college studying to teach special education. Keith and Bonnie plan to get married. They've been saying this since they were babies. I'm not one to judge. I have no plans at all.

"Shit," Keith says.

I mention a few variables that can affect a woman's cycle. I tell him to sit tight, don't worry, everything'll be fine. I'll bet she's not even pregnant. Things don't always have to turn out like shit. I don't feel good about saying any of this to him, but saying it gives me a kind of hope. I grab a mug off Keith's shelf, dump an inch of Tang in it, run it under the spigot in the sink, stir it with my finger, and sit on Keith's roommate's unmade bed, tangled in bedclothes, where I'll sleep tonight because he's gone for the weekend. Dirty clothes, papers, and food wrappers litter his side of the room. Books everywhere: pyramided on the desk and shelves, wedged into every niche available.

Keith tells me the roommate's a straight-A student, but a good guy. Randall. I walk over to Randall's closet and open it. There's a buckskin jacket with fringe hanging from the sleeves like Buffalo Bill's, boots, cowboy shirts with pearl snaps and embroidery. His jeans have different color braids sewn along the out-seams and cuffs. And more books: *The Doors of Perception, The Age of Reason, Stranger in a Strange Land, Future Shock.* Dozens more that I've never heard of.

"The first thing my mother did when they brought me up here was look through Randall's closet. She started bawling when she saw his clothes. 'Oh my God,' she's screaming at my dad, 'he's got a black roommate.' She'll have a stroke over Bonnie, Fritz. You know how she is. She'll blame it all on her."

Keith's right. Everything'll swing heavy against Bonnie.

I close the door to Randall's closet. "Let's shoot some pool," I suggest.

"Let's get high first."

Keith switches on his desk lamp, sits and opens the top drawer of his desk, pulls out a baggy of pot and rolls a number. His side of the room is immaculate. His few school books stacked on shelves along with a statue of Saint Anthony, instant coffee, sugar, Pream, and Cup-a-Soup. His desk just so. The candle and incense. A crucifix with a twisted-up Jesus above his manicured bed.

Keith's like some old Italian guy. He wears the horn around his neck to ward off the evil eye. Bites the back of his hand when he gets worked up. If he feels like it, he'll drop his head in his hands and weep. Tries to go to Mass and keep all the vigils and proper feasts. Still believes in the sacraments. Makes the sign of the cross every time he hears an ambulance. He possesses a soul I believe is spotless, and he is the closest thing I have to a brother, but sorry luck seems to betray him again and again. He confesses as we're smoking the joint that he and Bonnie were using the rhythm method.

Keith yanks out another baggy and holds it up in the light. Its golden contents glitter. When I don't say anything, he hands me the baggy. It's acid. *Sunshine. Orange barrels.* Roughly the size of an eraser on the end of a pencil.

"What are you doing with this?" I ask.

"Selling it."

"Why?"

"I need the bread."

"You're nuts."

He takes two barrels out of the plastic. "You want one?"

"Nope."

"Sunshine, Fritzy. Very mild."

"Uh-uh."

"Okay." He downs one with a swig of Tang, douses the light and blows out the candle.

We walk between two cliffs of plowed snow to the Student Union and rent a table. I'm no good at pool, but I like the random, the fact that those beautiful speeding balls on the table simply drop out of sight like magic. Keith can really play, and it comforts him to have the stick in his hand. To let his body for a moment lax out of that canter he's always in, his foot pounding time to some broken record.

Still, we talk about Bonnie and what if she's pregnant. Keith zips those balls into the pockets, calling each shot, each combination. Wielding that stick like a young man with a future ahead of him.

They'll get married right away. He'll quit school and sign on down at Homestead Steel or J & L Laborers on the open hearth make good money. He can hack that for a while. Until the baby is born. Then he can go back to school, maybe at night, if he wants.

"What are you talking about?" I ask. "Quit school?"

Keith's sighting down on the eight ball, drawing back to puncture the cue and end the game. His cigarette sags out of his mouth. Ashes fall onto the green tabletop as he lifts his head to look at me and say: "I'm flunking out."

The freedom did him in: he goofed around, didn't do anything he was supposed to do. Now, this last little bit, he's been too upset about Bonnie. He isn't going to pass anything. His mother and father'll hang him, then the Bonnie thing on top of that. Not to mention her parents who he's known all his life. Bonnie's put down a month's rent—sixty-five bucks, everything included—on an apartment above a flower shop on Penn Avenue. She and Keith are moving in together as soon as he gets back to Pittsburgh. That's why he needs the income from the acid. Getting married won't be such a bad move. A wife and baby. That's a beautiful thing.

He lays his hand on my shoulder and assures me that I'll be best man, the baby's godfather. He swears to God. If he can just bide through this tough spot he'll be a devoted husband, a great father. Have a little garden in the backyard and play bocce with his dad and grandfather down at the club yard on Sundays after Mass. Fridays he and Bonnie'll go to the Pleasure Bar for shots and beers and fish sandwiches.

I nod my head in punctuation. Why not shoulder that hod and get a head start humping it for life? A born sufferer, Keith possesses the constitution to pull it off. Not as a teacher—he'll never find his way back to school—but as some slob in green work fatigues shoveling slag for the county or stuck in some mill forever until asbestosis and cigarettes kick in.

Fluorescent lights drone above us like infinity, the eight ball stranded on the felt next to Keith's tiny mound of ash. I have to say something: my whole mission in traveling here is to deliver him, but there is nothing I, the soul of anonymity, can say. I can't even summon the energy to pretend that I have a future. Beyond the panel of windows we stand behind, students sled down the Union lawn on swiped dining hall trays.

Keith laughs. A desperate laugh. His head looks about to detonate, like his bandana is cinched one notch too tight and finally his conscience will spout out the top of his head. He's getting ready to cry. That's what it is. And I suddenly feel too stoned to cope with it.

"Let's thumb to West Virginia," I say.

Keith looks at me for a moment. His brassy pupils beam. Then his face becomes placid, as if of all the things I might have posed to comfort him, a trip to West Virginia is the correct choice.

"Okay," he says. "I'm up for that."

"Wheeling's not far. I think if we can get away for just a little bit, we can figure things out. And drink legal."

"Sounds good, Fritzy."

We catch a bus out of California, to the end of the line, a town called Lover, step onto Interstate 70 heading west, and stick out our thumbs. Out here on the big highway, the world is dark and abandoned. Freezing cold. The air we suck crackles. Wind snaps. Whatever is dropping from the sky clicks as it hits the stretched skin of Pennsylvania farmland. Phantom sedans with blacked-out interiors blow by. Taillights dwindling. We walk for a while in the direction of West Virginia. Snow falls in waves. It rolls across Pennsylvania, a great shroud of oblivion. Like time-lapse photography, we are up to our shins in it in minutes. The last car stumbles by and dissipates. The highway shuts down. We forget about Wheeling and trudge back into Lover.

The town proper is comprised of a train depot, Lowry's Café, a hardware store, a grocery store, post office, police station, and Saint Joseph's Catholic Church. Not another soul on the streets. With the snow trammeling down upon it, icing it in a somnolent reverie, Lover resembles something remembered. Not clearly real, but a dead child's play set. Frightfully old. Antique. Vanished. As if a curtain in time has parted for an instant and Keith and I have been thrown back through it. I know that I am lost, in all aspects of the word, but I don't let on to Keith, who literally vibrates with the speed buzz acid delivers.

This is just another notch in the gun, more proof that nothing makes sense, that God at a given moment can spit you right into a pile of shit. Keith looks at me imploringly, then simply plops down on the sidewalk across from the police station, pulling at his hair, chewing on his hands, getting off big-time now. On the downhill, speedballing, doesn't know how to stop, gnawing out the inside of his mouth, thinking about Bonnie, wishing he hadn't dropped that little barrel and ended up in this crazy vision.

Inside the police station, a portly cop, his hips heavy with equipment, putters about the small, brightly lit office. He talks on the phone; he pours coffee. He seems harmless enough, even kind. Out of sheer desperation, I want to ask him for help. Bus routes are suspended for the night and Keith is flipping. But, born with a mistrust for uniforms, I hunker down next to Keith and ask him what he wants to do. I have to get him up off the sidewalk. If that cop spies us, strangers, in our army jackets and jagged hair, our undisguised disarray, he'll come out and investigate. One look into Keith's kaleidoscopic eyes and we're busted.

When Keith pulls his hands away from his head, his fists are full of hair.

"I'm freezing to death, Fritzy. God is punishing me. He's going to bump me off right here in this one-horse hick town."

Keith's hair is a thorn bush ravaged with snow. His face is blue. I can't feel my fingers. Pentecostal snow storms down. The only other lit building is the church, across the street, half a block from the police station. A spotlight plays on Saint Joseph, the patron of fathers and working stiffs, in an alcove above the sanctuary doors. In his arms he holds the squirming Christ-child. "Get up, Keith," I command, and grab him by the arm.

"I need a cigarette bad, Fritzy."

"Get up."

He clambers to his feet and I hurry him across the street, up the steps of Saint Joseph's, and lean against one of the monumental doors.

"I'll be struck dead, Fritzy."

The door yields and we lurch inside. The church's only light shines from the banks of flickering red votive candles on the side altars. It breaks over the statues. Their shadows leap off the walls as if they are coming to life around us. Above the altar, a very shy Christ sleeps on his tree, aching for privacy, wishing that for this one night He could be left alone. Keith lights a cigarette and gapes up at the Savior.

"Alright, man," he says. To whom I'm not sure. I'm behind him with my hand in the holy water font.

"Bonnie wants to get an abortion," he chokes out, still with his back to me. The smoke from his cigarette finds its way into the candlelight. Tiny clouds of it flare up to the crucifix.

Jesus moves. Imperceptibly. The fingertips. His parched lips. An eyelid.

Keith says, "I want you to hear my confession, Fritzy."

He turns, and I see that he is crying. Tears streaming down his chapped blue face, the smoke corrugating his maniacal hair.

"Look," I say, raise my hands in front me, palms up, suppliant. Like: *This is just too much, Brother.*

"You, Fritzy. Right fucking now. I'm dying."

He's tripping at light speed now. The devil's horse. No reasoning. Crossed over.

"Okay," I tell him. "Go ahead."

"In the confessional."

"C'mon, Keith." I'm afraid of confessionals. Vertical coffins. Whispering black silence. Like a bad trip: your dead Italian ancestors mumbling in the cellar.

"Please, Fritz. My immortal soul. Life everlasting."

I walk to the confessional, open the door, take the purple stole from its nail inside, kiss it, and drape it sacramentally around my neck as I've seen priests do, then cross the ornately carved threshold, sit and let the door seal me in blackness.

An instant later, Keith enters the penitent's chamber. I hear him strike a match, smell the sulphur, then cigarette smoke. I slide back the screen and there he is: an apparition with writhing hair and hallucinogenic breath.

He says, "Bless me, Father, for I have sinned." He tells me that his last confession was months ago, that he has fallen away from the church. His soul is in peril. He has had premarital sex again and again with his girlfriend, Bonnie. She might be pregnant. They are contemplating abortion. *Murder*, he calls it.

I glance through the screen and make out the silhouette of his dazzled head, its faint earnest glow. I feel his guilt transfusing into me, hot, nerve-wracking. Jesus strains against the spikes pinning him to the cross. I'm waiting for His hushed voice in my ear, the one highlighted bloody red in the Gospels: *It's okay, Fritz. You didn't do a thing wrong. Forget about it.* The police are just beyond the church doors. Keith is spilling how much he loves Bonnie. More than anything. More than his mother. He'll fucking prove it: stick a knife through his head. *Gimme a knife, Fritzy.* Crying. Smoking so hard he's going to set the confessional on fire. Spontaneously combust. I read somewhere that sometimes people just catch fire. Walking down the street or sitting on the couch.

But it's me smoldering, really, in a big vat of sin.

Two days after Keith left for California, I stopped by Bonnie's house with some eight-tracks he asked me to return to her. We'd ride around summer nights and listen to them. The three of us in Keith's 1969 black Volkswagen Bug. Keith and Bonnie in the front, me in the back, the mossy third-world smell of hash, our wailing above the cheap vibrating speakers. *Blue. Live Rhymin'. Bookends. Tea for the Tillerman.* I'm still singing those songs. Under all the layers of what I seem to be, they still tell my story, maudlin and stuck, truncated like the town of Lover: an illusion, sweet as hell, and worth dying for.

But it was a dangerous summer too. A boy we knew jumped off the Meadow Street Bridge. A kid down on Spahr Street blew his head off in front of his best friends in a game of Russian roulette. The Pittsburgh fire captain, in thirty pounds of turnout gear, fell off a barge supervising Fourth of July fireworks over the clairvoyant Allegheny and drowned. The hoods down on Chookie's corner made their first overtures to heroin. I started working construction for my Uncle Pat: carrying a hod up and down dilapidated scaffold, treetop-high and threatening to collapse with every mincing step I took. Boys without futures have short names, short lives. That summer my name was fear, my address vertigo. I spent my shift begging God to keep me from falling.

In August, Keith split for college, went to California. Not the golden West Coast, but just an hour and a half down the road to a played out coal town at the end of a two-lane blacktop where kids from southwestern Pennsylvania with crummy college boards ended up by default to stay wasted on quaaludes and methadone, Alice Cooper, and Clint Eastwood westerns. Keith left me levitating four stories up with a cross of bricks on my back. But in the meantime, he and Bonnie had started that summer having sex, writhing among the VW stick shift, steering wheel, and bucket seats.

Keith still had dreams, but I'm not sure I did. I smoked two packs of cigarettes a day, and when I finally made it home after a day of laboring to the empty house I ate the meal my father had stacked in the oven for me, smoked some more and read Spiderman comic books till I passed out. Like a bum on a bum trip.

Toting the eight-tracks, dizzy from a day of working on a scaffold, a crust of mortar graying my sunburn, I came up on Bonnie through the tiny backyard, a patch of crabgrass and clover, that lurched off a narrow alley behind the apartment she lived in with her parents above Howard Kronzek's Butcher Shop on Margherita Street. Squads of big black flies buzzed over garbage drums stuffed with spoiled meat. The air stank of blood.

She was sunbathing, splayed out on a rusty chaise lounge. The blue and pink striped bikini, the strings untied. When she heard the gate rattle, she bolted upright, clutching at her breasts the way women do when surprised. Imperious, vulnerable, powerfully beautiful. There wasn't much sun to speak of, just a chromium sheen, the sky a chipped mirror. We had been locked for days in a heat wave. A blanket of pollution the steel mills asphyxiated the city with once or twice a summer. The weatherman called it an "inversion": grimy, noxious air trapped between the sidewalks and sweaty clouds of ore dust and carbon.

She stood in a shaft of dirty silver light, her body oiled, deep brown. Little beads of grease and sweat stood out like Hail Marys on a rosary. A strip of fabric across her chest, a patch between her legs. Tongues of heat flashed off her, rising up out of her scalp like another head of hair.

I told her I had the music from Keith. By then she had taken her hands away from her breasts, but hadn't bothered to retie the straps, which dangled down below her waist. Every so often a sweat bead ruptured and swept down her body. She said she was hungry. Did I want something to eat? She was about to head in to fix something when I showed up. She grabbed a T-shirt and yanked it on. I had nowhere to go. My mother and father would have already taken off for work. Sometimes I hated going home to an empty house. Yeah, I told her, I'll have something to eat. I wasn't thinking too much about anything, until she took my arm as we walked toward her back door.

Once inside, we were suddenly blinded. When we stepped out of the infrared glare of the inversion and into the house, everything turned pewter and sepia, preternaturally still, like we'd been suddenly inserted into a silent movie. Then a hood of vertigo dropped on me. Over my eyes, stuffed in my mouth and nostrils. My heart jackhammered. I began to sweat. Paralysis inched along my skin. When Bonnie asked what was wrong, I was unable to speak. I had begun dissolving, like a TV picture fading away into a milky, porous speck.

I must have panicked. I felt the bricks and mortar spraddle my back, the black speed of steel on ether. Blacking me out. Ponderous weight, then hush. Then I returned, sweating, propped in a chair, Bonnie gripping my hand, holding a water glass to my lips. Perhaps I said something. In my head it sounded like ventriloquism. We kissed. One kiss.

Holding my hand, she led me to the kitchen. She clamped her hair on top of her head with bobby pins. Sweat had seeped in horizontal stripes through her T-shirt. The backs of her legs were streaked with salt. I sat on a chair and watched her scramble eggs. She peeled cellophane wrappers off two pieces of yellow cheese and laid them on the eggs. Craning over the pan as she cooked, her shoulders narrowed, in one hand a spatula and in the other a cigarette.

I ate the eggs. She sat across from me, smiling and smoking cigarettes. When I finished eating, I lit up too. She hurried off to change. We were going to take a walk around the reservoir. Get out of there before her parents came home from work. I heard her in the bedroom, clothes whispering, then water running. I started after her. She wasn't beautiful, nothing like that picture on Keith's desk.

I need to say something to Keith, lay some kind of comfort on him. He's in his damn sorrow seat, heaving. The saints and mendicants around us leaving their pedestals, clopping like zombies over the stone floor of the sanctuary, pressing plaster ears to the confessional doors. I glimpse the future, clear as holy water. Keith's dad'll blow up and tell him he's a gold-plated loser. His mother'll cry. Then they'll forgive him and the whole thing'll fade. Even the passion that led to the baby: that glorious, sacramental fit of desperate, self-destructive sex. Bonnie's parents will poor-mouth and shamble and smile. They'll be glad it's Keith and not some gigolo from Larimer Avenue.

It's hard to say what I was thinking that blind afternoon at Bonnie's. I know I wanted a girl of my own, that I felt sorry for myself. More than anything I was scared to death. I stood in the dark hall beyond her opened door. Snared in the window's eerie light, wearing only a pair of white panties, she faced me as she struggled into a pair of jeans and snapped them, a sash of flesh pleated at the waistband. Her breasts were white as gypsum in relief against her burnt skin. Between them glinted the Miraculous Medal: the Blessed Virgin Mary draped in chiseled gowns of regal sorrow. Struck after the apparitions to Saint Catherine Labouré in 1830, the medal was favored by women. On it were notched the words: *O Mary conceived without sin, pray for us who have recourse to thee.* My mother owned one. It hung from her vanity mirror.

On Bonnie's dresser sat Keith's high school graduation picture: white shirt, tie, and dark coat, his hair trimmed, but one unruly wave rolling across his forehead and down over his right eyebrow, the left arched, long sideburns slicing along his jaw, an embarrassed, kind smile. Depending from a corner of the frame, the blue and gold tassel from his mortarboard.

If Bonnie saw me, she never let on. She turned her back, and there in the watery light, like a flash of lightning, was a scar. It traveled her backbone: nape of the neck to her jeans, where it ended in a tuft of dark down, like a mushroom cloud. Then I remembered. Seventh grade. The operation she had endured to correct a spinal defect. The body cast she lived in for six months. Our class, the entire school, prayed every day for her recovery, signed cards that Sister Saint John of the Cross sent twice a week. We collected money for the massive hospital bills her family could not afford. Throughout East Liberty, in the pharmacies and grocery stores and bars, there were pictures of Bonnie in her purple voile confirmation dress above handwritten pleas, then a jar for contributions.

One day Sister took us by bus down to Margherita Street to visit Bonnie in the four-room rental over Kronzek's. Advertisements in glyphic Yiddish mixed with English were posted on pink butcher paper to the enormous glass windows. Behind the counter, Mr. Kronzek, his long white apron splashed with blood, stabbed with a squat silver blade at a shoulder of bright red meat. A trestle of blood hung heavy, horrifically sweet and smoky, in the sky that draped his building.

All twenty-five of us trooped up the fire escape into the Guidas' clean, dingy kitchen, where Bonnie's parents greeted us with practiced deference, as if they were the schoolchildren. Her father's English had a hoarse, Calabrian creak. The mother's eyes were colorless, her hair a spongy ochre. When she spoke, she cried, so she hushed and smiled and offered us a tray of fancy cookies from the

Italian bakery while her husband held her elbow and looked at the yellow scuffed linoleum, glancing up occasionally to smile and nod his head, lift one hand and then the other to his thin, glistening black hair. Sister choreographed our every move with unblinking eyes and the snap of her fingers. We each took a cookie and smiled back, thanked the Guidas, lowered our eyes, then followed them single file down the gray hall to Bonnie's room.

All the cards we had sent were tacked to the wall above her hospital bed, horizontal bars along the sides and a crank at its foot. Above the cards, Jesus Christ Himself, in the throes of lonesome death, looking down from His cross upon Bonnie, spun in the thick white cocoon, arms and legs kneading the air like a beetle on its back, her hair chopped like a nun's, neck exaggerated. Everything exaggerated: her ruddiness, her smile, the sudden good cheer of her parents, Sister Saint John addressing her as "My child," the girls stepping forward to say hi and giggle, touching Bonnie's spidery hand, the boys knowing we should say something, but sidling into silence. The huge metal handle, screwed into the side of the cast, to lug Bonnie in and out of her bed. Keith stationed like a broken-down old man at the head of the bed.

We ringed her and Sister led us in the Our Father, Hail Mary, and Glory Be. Bonnie folded her hands on the bulbous breast of her cast and closed her eyes. Mrs. Guida cried. Mr. Guida smiled apologetically and patted her hand. Then we stepped up and autographed Bonnie's cast. We figured she was a goner, that we had gathered in requiem to say good-bye. Frighteningly beautiful, like an angel finally immured in inscribed plaster, Bonnie seemed ready for her listing in Butler's *Lives of the Saints.*

As we tripped from the room, Mrs. Guida, trying to thank us, began to weep in earnest. Her husband looked like he wanted to pull his eyes out. He attempted to voice his gratitude, but his crude English was so fractured with emotion that he simply stopped, covered his face for a moment, then turned to the cracked wallpaper and tapped his head over and over against it.

Sister, obviously agitated, clicking her fingers and hissing, herded us toward the door, all but Keith, still at Bonnie's bedside, his hand through the bars holding hers, whispering something as he tried not to cry, and she beaming as if already on the other side, among the Communion of Saints, conferring benediction.

Maybe, that afternoon I showed up at Bonnie's with the eight-tracks, it was seeing the scar. The scar and hearing again the sound of Mr. Guida's head knocking off the wall, his wife's choking sobs. That handle like a giant hook sticking out of Bonnie's side. And Keith, already, at age twelve, swallowed up by love and guilt and, like all of us, unable to distinguish between the two. I turned from Bonnie's bedroom, quietly retraced my steps back down the hall, then through the kitchen, and walked out of her house. I wanted to blame her for my betrayal of Keith, say she was a whore or something, but that wasn't true. She was a good thing. I was the whore. Whoring myself out to panic. One lousy kiss didn't mean shit. We were just friends. I had heard there were kids in East Liberty secretly writing books, hiding out in attics painting crazy pictures. To keep from jumping off a bridge.

When I see Bonnie these days, when Keith is home on weekends, I tell myself that that hour or so of incendiary longing four months ago burned me clean of something, but it still hangs there between Bonnie and me like an inversion. Suffocating air. I do what I've learned to do with pain: I don't think about it. Keith, on the other hand, thinks of nothing else. Right now, he's scratching at the gauze that separates us in the confessional, threatening to break through it and grab me by the throat.

Fornication, Fritzy. Murder and fornication.

I could condemn him to hell. Or exercise the power of absolution God has vested in me: tell him to go in peace and sin no more. At the very least I should tell him to run as fast and far as he can from the life he's about to stagger into. I begin to see in the dark. Not in the dark, but the darkness itself.

EPIPHANY

It was a long hike up to Highland Park Pond to ice skate, all the way to the top of Highland Avenue where two enormous angels with swords stood on granite plinths at the park entrance. The fountain had frozen, its silver spray lashed in midair like a little girl in her first Holy Communion dress. Even the reservoir had seized up, black ducks squatting in despair on the ice.

No one was out, the cold too ferocious for walkers and lovers, kids on swings and monkey bars, the old Italian men playing bocce. No visitors to the zoo. Along the park road, caribou and moose stood behind their cyclone fences, chuffing out clouds of smoke. Even the vagrants and boosters had disappeared, their old soldiers, cigarette butts, and syringes visible in the undressed bushes where they trysted with cheap dope and that first batch of girls who walked away from virtue to spite their immigrant parents.

I was on my own. Until my parents got home from their restaurant jobs at three in the morning, and by that time I'd be asleep; all the lights in the house on—something they never, even at the height of recrimination and vendetta, ever said a word about. Up there in the massive park, the pale day brittle, silent as glass, I felt safe. No one can hurt you when you are alone in the light; a ghost, even those of your tortured ancestors, can't bear the cold. Ill will withers in frigid temperatures.

The pond was over a steep hill through a black block tunnel sprayed with peace signs and derogations, littered with frozen rubbers and broken bottles; then through a grove of enormous sycamores. I dropped my skates at the base of a tree shaped like a pregnant woman, scraped a circle down to the dirt with my boot heel, snapped off low spindly branches for kindling, and got a fire going with wooden matches I struck on my teeth and a section of the *Post-Gazette* I had stuffed in my shirt.

The flames sprayed light off the sycamore's belly, parchment white and perfectly smooth where the bark had peeled away. From where I squatted, I could see the pond. In the wind, along its gray surface, skimmed eddies of fine snow. Beyond it was the public swimming pool, known as the Inkwell because the black people had taken it over. It cost a quarter for kids to get in. My mother didn't allow me to swim there. She claimed I'd get a disease. I half believed her, but I went anyhow. My dad didn't care, but he avoided arguing with her if he could help it. The pool was drained. A foot of snow sat in the guard chairs at either end.

When the fire was in no danger of going out, I unzipped my jacket, reached under my sweater, and took a square of wax paper out of my shirt pocket. Wrapped in it were five strips of bacon, which I draped over a stick and held above the fire. I had also brought along whiskey siphoned from my parents' half gallon of Black Velvet into an empty baby food jar—strained peaches, the chubby Gerber baby smiling at me from the label—I had discovered, along with several others, under the kitchen sink.

The bacon turned translucent. Grease ran down the stick and dripped cracking into the fire. The whiskey gagged me. I poured it out, leaving an amber funnel in the deep snow. I ate the bacon, still slightly raw, before it crisped. Took off my jacket, spread it on the snow, then sat on it and smoked one of the cigarettes I had swiped from the packs lying around the house. Pall Malls, long and tight, filterless, sweet after the bacon and scalding whiskey.

There came a long, low rumble like far-off thunder. But nothing like thunder: caged lions roaring inside the big block fortress where they wintered. Out of reflex, I glanced around, lit another cigarette.

When I was a little boy, a lion had somehow escaped from the zoo. For three days, it was at large before it appeared, lapping water from a dock along the Allegheny River, and was shot with tranquilizer darts by the river patrol. For a while after that, I had nightmares. A lion in the house, prowling toward my bedroom, his roar vibrating my bed, shaking me out of sleep. Then the roaring stepped inside me, stealing my breath so that I couldn't even cry out, but lay staked on my shivering bed as the lion padded up the linoleum hall. I'd pray as I had been taught, but that never stopped the door from nosing open inch by inch. Then I smelled him: the musk and heat, the man-eating indifference. The wallpaper, by glow of the nightlight, writhed with his hulking, muscled shadow. Then the breath and slavering as he reached out to me with his claws. And it would hit me then that I was cursed. Otherwise he would never have decided upon me, of all the children in Pittsburgh.

I would attempt to tell my parents this, to describe every nuance, as they rushed into my room, but by then I was snarled inside my own scream, and it would take every light burning throughout the house, every impossible promise and assurance my parents could fabricate, before I could catch my breath and allow them to convince me that I had not been ripped to pieces. That it had been merely a dream.

My father carried me downstairs against his naked chest. At his side, my mother, wearing only my father's shirt, held my hand in her soft hand, and he laid me on the couch. In the first few hours of morning. Often they had just come home from work. The very last of TV sputtering: the civil defense logo and a score by Henry

Mancini, then the national anthem, followed, until daybreak, by convulsing white lines and hissing. Corned beef sandwiches in white delicatessen paper, beer in squat Iron City bottles, shot glasses and a fifth of VO on the coffee table. The smoke from their cigarettes, docked in a giant turquoise ashtray shaped like a scallop shell, furled into limbo like interrupted sentences.

My mother, still with my hand in hers, told me that this year she would make me with her own hands the grandest Halloween costume: Zorro. And that would get me to smile, even then knowing that she could barely sew a button on, and that of course, we'd buy a packaged costume at Murphy's—a buccaneer or the devil—and that for the school party, I would be Saint Frederick, my patron saint, a bishop martyred in 838 A.D.: a burnt cork beard, my bathrobe, and a towel on my head.

But that mattered little on those nights I had been spared. I could see clearly into my mother's heart: she loved me in an inconsolable way that permitted her to lie and even hurt me sometimes. My dad sat there clairvoyantly, his hand in my hair, his eyes on my mother, shaking his head at her in wry admiration. I always watched him when he looked at her, and even when he was goaded into anger, even when he wanted to bash her just to shut her up, he loved her. Loved her furiously, like those junkies down on Chookie's corner loved junk. And I always knew he loved me. Always.

They gave me their pickles and some of their cheesecake. My dad let me toast marshmallows over the stove's gas burners. I'd fall asleep playing five-card stud with my mother and father, gambling Wise potato chips, Nat King Cole on the hi-fi, me singing along to "Mona Lisa" in what I thought was a perfect imitation of his voice. My parents laughing, looking at each other as if they were keeping something from me, fading into the still black night like apparitions.

I'd wake up in their bed, the circumspect light of morning coating everything in inevitability: my father's snore; my mother, mouth open, in a black velvet sleep mask like the ones Dorothy Kilgallen and Arlene Francis wore in *What's My Line*, bare-shouldered, black stubble under her arms, hay-colored hair beaten into the purple pillowcase.

I'd get dressed, eat a bowl of Cheerios, grab milk money and the lunch my father had packed—*Fritz* scrawled hieroglyphically on the brown bag—and trudge to school. They'd be awake by the time I got home.

Four o'clock, maybe. The sun, in an envelope of pewter clouds, hung low over the reservoir. I stood, threw on my jacket, and pissed on the fire. It sizzled and smoked. I kicked a mound of snow over it until it died completely, grabbed my skates, and hurried toward the pond. It was abandoned, as if no one knew it existed. The entire park seemed abandoned. Early January. Winter in Pittsburgh so interminable after Epiphany—the three kings at last in Bethlehem—that to ponder spring too soon was self-destructive. I sat on the bank and struggled into the stiff hockey skates. Maroon with black toe, tongue, and laces, they rose just over my ankle, the dull silver blades heavy and thick.

My dad scored the skates for almost nothing from Jimmy, the dishwasher at the Park Schenley where my dad worked as a waiter. The skates were *hot.* Stolen. My parents often purchased hot items: cigarettes, Canadian whiskey and VO, wristwatches, lightbulbs. My dad once brought home an entire set of china, complete service for eight—*Wedgewood*—but it sat in its crate behind the sofa until my mother blew up one night and busted it all to hell.

What I had really wanted were figure skates, black mid-calves with black laces; but my dad didn't know the difference and Jimmy's car trunk was loaded with hockey skates and the slashed price was too sweet to pass up. Skates were skates.

I stepped onto the scarred ice and pushed off, my strokes short and choppy. I hadn't been skating long, but I rarely fell, and once going I could cut along with considerable speed. The ice, along the pond's perimeter, was slushy, and in places a fringe of water lapped. I had the sensation that the vast plane upon which I skated tipped with my weight and, without dwelling on it, I envisioned it splitting apart and me bobbing among the floes until my heavy skates, like anchors, bore me down to the catfish and carp dreaming on the pond's mud floor.

The light was fading: gray on gray on gray, then probably more snow. Jackdaws plumped in the spiked top branches of the trees surrounding the pond. They'd chitter, then hush to utter stillness. When one left a tree, the others spooled up too, black as the priest's biretta.

The ice had a way of whispering, then yawing like a bow skidding over a fiddle. You couldn't tell where the sound came from, but it seemed locked just below the frozen surface. The wind picked up, my eyes nearly chapped shut, my tongue circling the last layer of skin on my lips, tasting the blood leaking through the cracks. I whipped over the dingy ice until the light was merely a skullcap over the reservoir. My feet began to cramp. I was sweating under my clothes, hungry. Maybe it had begun to snow. I couldn't tell, but my face was wet.

I skated to the bank and stepped onto it over the ice's edge where the slush sluiced up. Something was in the narrow sleeve of water. There wasn't much light, but I could clearly make out a face. A little kid, maybe a first or second grader, floating, in a brown jacket and cap. His eyes were open. I was old enough to know what to do, but there was no one around. No phones. No cars. The last scraps of daylight lingered in the snow, like those icons that glow in the dark after the lamp is snuffed. I heard the rumbling of those big cats again. The ice shimmied like it was breaking apart. I reached down and grabbed the kid by his lapels.

THE HIGH HEART

Three days after Christmas, and I was at the poker table along with Seymour and McCafferty at Keith Gentile's.

Keith had had a plenty rough day, most of it spent with his girlfriend Bonnie in an abortion clinic down in Oakland. You could see how frayed he was. Skinny as hell and that big head of electrocuted hair, one cigarette after another and the veins in his blue forehead like hot wires about to rupture. Every so often he'd interrupt the game to get up and check on Bonnie who was asleep in his bedroom. Then he'd drag back in that baggy Captain America shirt and bells way too short, and throw me a worried glance, tears in his eyes, then try to get back in the game.

I had chipped in to help pay for the abortion, and had gone along with them to the clinic. Keith wanted to keep the baby, but Bonnie insisted they shouldn't have children until they were married. Keith still had religion, and worried it was murder, an unpardonable sin. Something he and Bonnie would be tormented by, a curse laid on them by God, for the rest of their lives. Bonnie didn't say a word. She kissed Keith, walked into the room with the nurse, and the door closed behind her.

Sitting next to Keith on a hard wooden bench, I had tried to put out of my mind what was going down on the other side of the white clinic wall against which we leaned. While we waited, the darkness of the winter streets beyond the window threw a hood over the afternoon, and then the light shut down completely.

We were playing a game McCafferty introduced, called High Heart. Straight seven stud, but to win, for the game to finally end, somebody had to catch not only the high hand, but also—and this was the kicker—the highest heart on the table as one of his three down cards. The betting got nuts because a guy sitting on the ace, king, queen of hearts, or even a lower heart underneath, would drive things up hoping to catch a decent hand or at least bluff people out. The same held true for someone who landed big cards early. He'd bet like he had it and pray for a heart on the last down card.

If someone couldn't parlay both high heart and high hand, the cards were shuffled and another round dealt. Fold, and nobody wins the hand, you're done. You sit out the rest of the game. You either get out in a big hurry, or stay in because so much of your money is sitting there in front of you on the table and you can't bear to let it go. A sucker game: greed, stupidity, and what passed for guts.

I folded early. I simply couldn't afford to stick it out, but Keith, round after round, like Russian roulette, like he had a pistol to his temple, hung with Seymour and McCafferty. He had this dogged, doomed look on his face, like he had been forsaken by free will and all that remained was to toss his money onto the table and run back and forth to his bedroom and check on Bonnie.

"Hey, Keith, will you please pay attention?" Seymour said.

"Sorry."

"It's to you. A bean."

"Man," Keith said, and threw a dollar into the pile of bills and change in the middle of the table.

"Drop, if you don't have the stomach for it," cracked McCafferty.

I looked up, but said nothing. I hadn't known McCafferty very long; he was a friend of Seymour's from college and occasionally showed up at the poker games, so I had no way of telling if he was serious or kidding. McCafferty was a little too slick. The way he throttled the deck like a sharp and dealt, snapping off the cards between his thumb and middle finger and twirling them across the felt: *bullets* and *ducks*, *johnnies* and *cowboys*, *boats*, *all silk*, *twenty miles of track*. McCafferty with his movie lines like: *Drop, if you don't have the stomach for it.* Like this was some very dire scene. Like he was Doc Holliday. Like the whole backdrop of Keith's apartment, his furniture, and his friends existed only to showcase what a miraculous character he was.

The hell with you, I thought. McCafferty was Seymour's friend. I wasn't going to worry about it.

McCafferty had his girlfriend with him. Just home from a vacation in Jamaica, they were dark brown from the Caribbean. The girl's name was Helen Munson. McCafferty called her Munson. The island sun had dropped a crown of light in her brown hair. Her nose and cheeks were cherry pink where she had peeled. Not a speck of makeup. Just her eyes and bleached brows, lashes, lips, a white dress with nothing under it. All that and she wasn't pretty. I found myself studying her for whatever flaw it was that ransacked her beauty.

She perched on the couch across the room pulling clumps of green marijuana out of a Giant Eagle grocery sack, breaking it up on a screen with a wooden frame around it, sluicing the shake into baggies, then lining the quarter-ounce cylinders side by side on the coffee table. She looked up only to hit the bong when it came her way.

McCafferty claimed they had smuggled the weed out of Montego Bay. Intermittently he'd lapse into a Jamaican patois. He called the reefer *ganga* and the bong the *chalese*. Joints were *spleefs.* He was the *heavy mon,* the *tilley mon.* Instead of drinking beer, he sipped from an unlabeled bottle he said was Jamaican overproof rum.

"I got too much invested in this to drop," Keith said, trembling slightly, zipping out another smoke and giving McCafferty the eye. I wanted Keith to fold, send everyone home, crawl in bed with Bonnie and sleep through the night without waking up once. The nurse had told them she'd be better the next day. They should have forgotten about poker, but it was a standing ritual, and Keith thought it would take his mind off things.

"It's bad luck to count the till, Rasta," McCafferty said, then laughed. He wore a top hat and had a beard. His eyes gleamed. He took a swallow of rum.

"I wasn't counting the till," Keith said.

"I know you weren't. I was just saying."

"Just play," said Seymour.

"My bet, I believe," said McCafferty.

Munson handed him the packed bong. It was made of clear glass the size of a softball. McCafferty puckered his lips into the shaft, Munson lit the bowl with a disposable, and he sucked mightily. The water boiled. The belly of the bong clouded with thick white smoke, roiling for an instant before he let off the carburetor with his pinky and all those shadows stormed down his throat. Munson pressed her mouth to his and, as they kissed, McCafferty blew the hit into her. She staggered back, gave a little shimmy and yelp, and let out a long jet of smoke, first from her mouth, then through her nose until the entire table shrouded.

"Two *dollah,*" McCafferty sang and passed the bong to Seymour.

"I don't know," Seymour said. "Let me hit this thing and ponder."

"I'll be right back," Keith said, and jumped up.

"One minute, Rasta. You're not going anywhere. There's a bet on the table," McCafferty said.

Keith looked at him, dumbfounded.

"I'm just kidding. Relax. We'll be here when you get back."

Keith stared at McCafferty another second, then strode out of the room. I got up and followed him.

Keith knelt at Bonnie's bedside, a double mattress on the floor, above which a crucifix hung. A black light shed a smoky glow. On the walls were posters of Janis Joplin and Jimi Hendrix. A radiator under the lone window hissed. Across the street was a convent, the Little Sisters of the Poor, and next to it a home they ran for old people. On the convent lawn, fronting the avenue, was a big Christmas tree with blinking red and green electric bulbs that splashed the ceiling of Keith's room. Bonnie, covered to the waist, snored lightly. She wore one of Keith's flannel shirts. Her beige hair was knotted in a long pigtail.

"I think she's running a fever, Fritz. Come and feel her."

I knelt next to Keith and placed my hand on Bonnie's forehead. It was warm and a little wet. She said something. *Maybe. Baby.* I couldn't tell. Her breath smelled like water left too long in a vase of flowers.

"What did she say?" Keith asked.

"I don't know."

"I'm worried, Fritz. I think she's hot. What do you think?" He put his hand again to Bonnie's forehead.

"I can never tell just by feeling. She's a little warm, but this room's like a furnace."

"You think I should turn the heat down?"

"I think it's okay."

"What if she has a fever?"

"What did the nurse say?"

"She said that's not unusual."

"Okay, then. Nothing's wrong."

"What if she dies, Fritzy?" Keith sat on the edge of the mattress and ripped at his hair.

"Listen, Keith." I laid my hand on Keith's shoulder. "Look at me, man." Keith looked up, his eyes red, tears falling down his face. "She is not going to die. You gotta get hold of yourself. She's going to wake up tomorrow and everything's going to be fine."

"I know, man. I know. But I keep feeling like all this is going to come back on me. I mean, Jesus Christ, Fritz." He lowered his face to his hands again. "I'll tell you one thing. I'm gonna kill that motherfucker in the other room next time he says a word."

"Forget about him."

"I'm telling you, Fritz, so when it happens you'll remember I told you."

"Look, you're a wreck over Bonnie. This whole thing. Go in the other room and fold, get the hell out of that game, last hand, everybody goes home, you go to bed, and everything'll be better tomorrow."

"Fold?"

"Yeah."

"With all my money in the pot? Just give it to that son of a bitch?"

"Yes."

"I'm busted, Fritz. Every nickel I had went into that Black Mass today. I can't afford to lose another cent."

"Then drop out of the game, and get that asshole out of your house. I can spot you a little bread. Fold."

"You think so?"

"I know so."

"Okay. I'll fold." Keith kissed Bonnie on the forehead. "You think she's alright?"

"She's fine, Keith. I wouldn't lie to you about it. I care about her too."

"I'm tired, man. I'm gonna fold."

"Good."

Reggae played and Munson danced trance-like, as if a light wind were cutting her languidly about the living room. Her thick hair vined across her face and, when she dipped and threw her head back, I saw that her breasts were brown too, that she didn't shave under her arms.

McCafferty handed the bong to Keith and laughed.

"I'm gone, man," Seymour said.

"You out?" Keith asked.

"Yep."

I looked at Keith. He had a ten and a pair of deuces showing. McCafferty had nothing but a smear of unrelated face cards. They each had two cards coming. One up. One down.

"I got him beat on the board," Keith whispered to me, then fired up the bong.

"Two bucks to you," McCafferty said to Keith.

Keith slid two dollars into the pot and knocked his beer off the table. I thought I heard a little cry from Keith's bedroom. Behind him Munson swayed, the revving music getting ready to blow them all hot out into the frozen night. I could smell her. Coconut. Sun-blanched skin. The taste of sea salt on my tongue. I had never seen the ocean. She was like some kind of temptress, seductive in a way that made her unbelievable.

The drapeless window in Keith's living room crusted with frost. Outside, the air crystallized, twisting itself around the streetlamps and convent lights. The concrete iced. Bits of gravelly snow chipped out of the sky.

"Turn that music down," Keith said. "Bonnie's trying to sleep."

Munson glided over to the stereo and lowered the volume. She stopped dancing and sat down at the table. I felt her radiating in the chair between me and McCafferty. Blessed warmth. Sunshine. Not the endless icy gray wall of Pittsburgh's winter. I wanted to touch her. Just touch her. She laid her head down on her arms and closed her eyes. McCafferty lifted a hank of her hair and let it fall through his fingers.

"The Stones did a concert in Kingston while we were there," McCafferty said. "Jagger almost caused a riot."

"What the hell does that have to do with anything?" Keith snapped. He pulled another beer out of the bag at his feet.

"Atmosphere, Rasta. Just thought you'd like to know," McCafferty came back.

"I'll raise you a couple more, Rasta," Keith said and laid two more bucks in the heap.

Seymour whistled. I spun a look at Keith. He looked dead back at me.

"Fuck it, you know. Just fuck it," Keith growled.

"Some fatalistic dread, mon," lilted McCafferty. He held two bills above the pot and let them fall.

"Deal," Keith ordered.

McCafferty ravelled off the ace of clubs to Keith.

"Bullet," he called. Then to himself a two. "Your deuce. No help. Your bet, Rasta."

Keith split off a five-dollar bill and threw it in. "Five bucks."

"Okay, Rasta. I'll see that five and raise it ten." McCafferty laid the money in, pulled a joint from behind his ear and lit it.

"That's a little extreme, McCafferty," Seymour said.

"What?"

"I don't know, man. A ten-dollar bump in a friendly game?"

McCafferty, bobbing his head to the music, took a three-beat hit on the joint, smiled, looked at everyone in turn, moored his eyes on Keith, then exhaled. "I'll retract the bet if it's too rich for your blood."

"Listen . . ." Keith started.

"This is bullshit, Keith," I interrupted. "Throw in your hand. You're getting sucked in."

"Really, Keith," Seymour seconded. "Don't blow any more money to this jagoff. You know, you're a jagoff, McCafferty."

"Throw in your hand, Rasta, and we'll call it a night."

Keith scattered another five and five ones into the middle.

The last cards came down.

Keith very deliberately slid his to the edge of the table, put his eye on the uplifted card corner. McCafferty picked up his card, blew on it, put it back down on the table, and smiled at Keith. "Your bet, Rasta."

"I'll check."

"Crafty, Rasta. It'll cost you one Old Hickory to see what I got under here."

"Twenty bucks, McCafferty? You're a real jagoff. This is a friendly game," Seymour spat.

"There are no friendly games, mon."

"Just fuck you," Seymour said.

"Man," I barked, and jumped up.

Keith looked at me, a cigarette twitching between his teeth as he talked, smoke catching like fog in his insane hair: "I'm going to see his bet, Fritzy. I'm not going to get run outta my own house by this fucking ramrod."

"You're nuts," I said.

Keith kicked in the twenty. "Alright, whatta you got?" But before McCafferty could answer, Keith turned over his cards and blurted, "I got deuces and tens, with the jack of hearts underneath."

McCafferty grinned at him for a moment, the same stagy awareness of every move he made, then began turning over cards one by one. He had two queens underneath to ride along with the one he had showing. One of them was the queen of hearts, prim, androgynous, judgmental. Trip queens with the high heart. McCafferty's pot. A hundred bucks easy. More.

Keith said nothing. He stared down at his cards on the table. He touched them as if they were braille, like they might suggest to him a better strategy or shape-shift into a higher hand.

"No," he said.

"No what?" answered McCafferty.

"You didn't win that hand."

“Well, where I come from, Rasta, three of a kind beats two pair every single day of the week. And a queen is higher than a jack.”

McCafferty looked at Keith and Seymour, then back to Keith. He dragged the money toward him.

“You did not win that fucking hand,” Keith said and stood up. McCafferty was smoothing the paper money, peering intently at each bill as he stacked it.

“C’mon, Keith,” Seymour said. “You know, c’mon. Forget about it.”

“This son of a bitch,” Keith shouted, pointing at McCafferty, who still had not looked up.

“Let it go, Keith. Forget about it,” I said.

Keith flicked his lit cigarette at McCafferty. It hit him in the chest, spraying red his sweater and the green tabletop with sparks. McCafferty looked up at Keith.

“He cheated,” Keith said, lunging with a finger at McCafferty’s face.

“C’mon, Keith,” Seymour said. “Nobody cheated. You lost the hand.”

“Look,” McCafferty said, still looking at Keith. “I’m going to pretend like I didn’t hear that accusation. That my favorite sweater didn’t just get mutilated by a lit cigarette hurled at me. I’m going to make a conciliatory suggestion. Why don’t we all load up and get something to eat at Finnegan’s? Forget about all this unpleasantness? My treat. Whatta you say, Rasta?”

“You fucking cheated, and you know it,” Keith yelled. “You are not taking that money out of this house.”

“Fighting words, Rasta.”

“Look, there’s no fighting going on here at all. Why don’t you just take your money and split, McCafferty,” said Seymour. He stood up. “Come on, let’s go. We’re all leaving.”

McCafferty remained rooted in his poker chair, his eyes blazing into Keith. Crazy Keith standing there shivering, another cigarette already in his blue lips, eyes like cracked lemon drops, his clothes pulling on his sharp, bony body.

"Can't leave now, Sey. There's another bet on the table. Laid down by this righteous Rasta here. This *heavy mon* signifying in my direction. Very high stakes."

"Give it a break, McCafferty. Just go home," Seymour pleaded.

"Son of a bitch cheated me, Seymour," shouted Keith.

"I didn't cheat."

"Fuck you didn't."

"Take it easy, Keith," I said.

Munson suddenly lifted her head and spoke to me: "I wish you would quit staring at me."

It dawned on me at that instant: Munson's flaw. Why she wasn't pretty. She was simply too unapproachably beautiful, too unattainable. As if it were her due, she carried around with her the sun. Temperate weather. Blue warm water. She possessed a genetic perfection that canceled out mutts like me and Keith. Like Bonnie lying split and bled back there in Keith's bedroom. Futures no longer than the walk from Keith's beat-up VW to the abortion table. I suddenly hated Munson for her ease within her skin, the guarantee she received from the mirror every morning when she gazed into it. McCafferty too. His confidence. His beauty. His good luck. His high heart. Munson was right. All night I had been staring at her, mesmerized by her breathtaking perfection, trying to find something wrong with her so I could dismiss her from my longing—as if I couldn't bear beauty because I wasn't worthy of it.

I was suddenly ashamed of everything: my home, my mother and father, my entire being. I saw my life as a succession of hourly wages that would keep me poor and sorry, as though it had all come down to this moment of Keith's knowingly false accusation and my inability to stand up and tell the truth. Keith and I. We'd rather die than tell the truth, admit how empty everything was, what losers we were. Stupid East Liberty kids whose only mode of dealing was to call someone out, true or not, then take a beating—death if it came down to it—and call it honor.

"Honey," said McCafferty, "he's been looking down your dress all night."

"You know, McCafferty," I answered. "I been holding off saying this, but you're the scum of the earth. What you came in here and did tonight."

McCafferty turned to me. "What is this Wild West shit? I cheated? Your nervous friend here is lying. Whatta we do? Slap leather?" Then to Keith: "Whatta you want to do, Rasta? You know I didn't cheat. You just have a bug up your ass because I tore your house down tonight. Now I'm going to stuff my pockets with your money that I won fair and square, and I'm walking out of here. You follow me, and I will hand you your second ass-whipping of the night. My advice is you crawl back to your soiled sheets and pussy and chalk this up to shitty cards. Better luck next time."

"Outside, motherfucker. Outside," Keith screamed, and threw his beer. The can whizzed by McCafferty's head and busted up the turntable. The record screeched, then died. Munson let out a little cry and laid her hand to her breast.

Keith's face looked like baby snakes were writhing just beneath his pink, bluish, mottled skin. "And I want this *puttana* out of my house," he said, jabbing a finger at Munson.

"What does that mean?" she asked.

"Some wop word," McCafferty said.

"What's it mean?" she asked again.

"What's it sound like it means, you fucking whore?" Keith yelled.

"You awful ugly thing," she said to Keith.

McCafferty stood up. He was tall and thick, smiling beneath his blond-streaked beard and silky black hat, blonde hair piling out beneath it. A long necklace of fat orange beads fell from his neck. "I'll gladly go outside with you, Rasta."

Keith started for the long, steep flight of stairs that led down to the street. Holding to the banister, he stumbled a few times on his way down. McCafferty was directly behind him, then Munson and I. Seymour called from the top of the stairs: "I'm going to call the cops."

The avenue was deserted except for a band of kids sledding down an adjacent side street. The snow had turned to sleet. It needled down, clicking off the frozen crust of snow and ice that covered everything, visible in the streetlamps and in relief against the convent Christmas tree each time the lights flashed. No cars. It was almost two in the morning.

Keith walked out to the middle of the avenue. He and McCafferty faced each other. The others stood around them shivering. No one had bothered with coats.

"I want to hear him say he cheated," Keith said.

"I didn't cheat," McCafferty said. "And you know it."

"I want to hear you say it before I kick your ass."

McCafferty hadn't cheated. Keith was all to hell over Bonnie, over the sorry turn his life was taking. All he knew, drunk and stoned as he was, was lie and swagger. I knew to step in, and tell the truth. Save Keith a beating. But the truth amounted to calling Keith a liar. Betraying my friend. I was stuck with Keith's version of saving face. I stood there silently, pricked by the freeze knifing down on me as Keith took a wild swing at McCafferty, then lost his balance and crashed into the frozen street. He clambered up, his head cut at the scalp line, and immediately lost his footing again. He lay there for a moment before pushing himself up again off the ice, buttons of blood falling from his head every few seconds as though precisely measuring time.

"Let's forget about it now, Keith," I said, clamping Keith under his arms and helping him to his feet.

McCafferty stood there expressionless. "It's over, Rasta." Munson, her bare arms folded across her chest, sidled against him. He wrapped an arm around her. The convent porch light flashed on. The kids, their sleds trailing them by wash twine, had milled over to watch.

I had an arm around Keith's waist. "C'mon, man. That's enough now. Okay?"

Keith nodded. He was crying, openly, unabashedly, tears and blood washing down his face. He slipped, righted himself, then whipped a fist at McCafferty. It caught Munson in the face. She screamed and went down, taking McCafferty with her. He jumped up, leaving Munson sitting in the street cupping the blood from her cracked nose, and in the same motion caught Keith twice in the mouth, a right and a left, then a knee until Keith balled down on the ice, heaving, McCafferty riding him, boots and fists, a long inventory of retribution, the wages of sin.

An old nun, in just wimple and plaid bathrobe, hurried out of the convent and teetered across the ice toward them. The children took off. Police sirens screeched in the distance.

I saw how wrong it all was: good intentions gone bad. The love between Keith and Bonnie, the abortion, the poker game, the egotism that pushes men to lie rather than admit pain and frailty and wrongdoing. My own inability to look in the mirror and see myself.

Still, I couldn't help it. Not for the nun, like the queen of hearts, scolding, "Young man," pulling at McCafferty, who kept pounding Keith. Not even when Bonnie, homely and small, a child who had had a child raked out of her that very morning, limped down the long staircase and fell to her knees, whimpering a sing-song litany of *please* and *Keith* over and over. Not for the boys in Vietnam dying instead of me, nor the poor souls in purgatory. I simply could not help it. In the glory of my imperfection, I blindsided McCafferty, knocking him clear of Keith.

Then suddenly it was me, back against the frozen earth, McCafferty's fists reminding me that I was beholden to a merciless planet, as Keith, sobbing *Jesus Christ*, crawled into Bonnie's arms where she rocked him like a child.

KILLERS

After Martin Luther King was murdered in the dry spring of 1968, the black people up on Herron Avenue, the part of town called the Hill District, a place few white people had ever set foot, looted and set fires. There came talk they were marching down off the Hill with torches, guns, and knives to lay waste to all of Pittsburgh. Smoke plumed out of neighborhoods across the city. Shrieking fire trucks and police cars tore through the streets. The mayor officially imposed a curfew. Most businesses, including the restaurants my parents worked in, temporarily suspended business until it was lifted.

My father, who had been to the Hill to listen to jazz and blues with some black guys he was tight with from work, said there was nothing to fear. You couldn't much blame the blacks for raising hell. Things would blow over soon enough. Nevertheless, like a lot of the men on our street, he borrowed a pistol: a gleaming blue-steel, snub-nosed .38, a sight at the barrel tip like a dorsal fin, and polished scrolled walnut handle. By day it rested in the nightstand drawer along with the Dr. Spock baby book, savings bonds, and my birth and baptismal certificates.

Come nightfall, my father took it up in his right hand and maintained vigil in the shadows of our front stoop. The only light on the block shone from the cigarettes of the other fathers on their porches and the corner streetlamp. All the houses were blacked out. I stayed inside with my mother. Clutching a foot-long bread knife, she crouched at an upstairs bedroom overlooking the street and said Hail Marys.

The gun was her idea. My father was not a man of action, but someone who wanted to get along, to be left alone. He had never done a blessed thing to offend a black person in his life; he treated them the way he'd treat anyone, with a friendly, warm indifference, and he felt this fact protected him from their retribution. My mother told him he was a fool and a coward. He'd stand by while those animals broke into the house and cut us all to pieces. Dressed in a chenille, wine-colored housecoat half-unbuttoned, she smoked cigarettes, ate cottage cheese, and drank coffee drilled with whiskey. He'd sit on his ass while they raped her.

"You're hardly their type, Rita," he cracked.

"Kiss my ass, Travis," her standard rejoinder, flecks of cottage cheese on her red lipsticked mouth. "What the hell happens when they're standing on our porch? What the hell are you going to do to protect Fritzy and me, you gutless wonder?"

My father had been predicting revolution for a while. He'd smack the newspaper with the back of his hand and say, "Hold onto your hat, Fritzy." When President Johnson announced he would not run for president, my father declared that Nixon, "God forbid," as he said, would be our next president.

"Nixon's a sneaky bastard," pronounced my mother. "All you have to do is look at him."

Four days after LBJ gave it up, James Earl Ray shot Martin Luther King in Memphis. My dad tried to explain that King was the black Jesus. He spun Mahalia Jackson spirituals on our hi-fi. And Billy Eckstine and Billy "Sweet Pea" Strayhorn, two famous black musicians he had gone to school with at Westinghouse

High. He had let his hair creep over his collar and the tops of his ears, and grown long sideburns. Sometimes he smoked marijuana. My mother worried about him. She hid the newspaper. It was filling his head with garbage. She called him a hophead, a nigger lover, who traipsed off to those ratty jazz clubs on the Hill with Jimmy, his big fat black friend who washed dishes at the Park Schenley. When especially pissed off, she'd say my father was queer; why else would he be loafing with that fairy lard ass *tizzone* dope fiend dishwasher? My dad would turn up the music. He had some old Charlie Parker that I really liked: everything frayed and letting go at once while you just kept flying, never landing, but you knew the crash was coming. I smelled hemp on my father, or maybe it was the charred air settling over the neighborhood.

The tide of black rage rolled toward East Liberty, lapping at our little one-way street. We had heard that the cops were shooting it out with the Black Panthers, that the Sears, a few blocks away, had been ransacked and was on fire. The National Guard had been mobilized. Down on the corner of Larimer and Meadow, a fifty caliber machine gun had been set up by the Sons of Italy on the second-storey roof of Johnny and Carlo's Dairy.

"Let's take a walk, Fritzy," my father said. "Bum around the Avenue a bit."

"Like fun. There's a war out there," my mother countered. Lighting cigarette after cigarette, she slumped at the living room window peering out into the street. "I don't want to be left alone."

"Rita, we wouldn't abandon such tempting prey to those savages."

My mother sprung off the couch and draped herself across my father's back. "Don't you dare leave this house, Travis." She ran her hands up under his T-shirt.

"I'm not going anywhere."

But I wasn't so sure. I was always afraid my dad would walk out.

"I couldn't live without you, Travis. You're a killer."

When he turned around, she kissed him wildly.

"I bet you could," he said when she finally uncoiled from him.

Sometimes I'd sneak in and open the nightstand drawer. I never touched the pistol. Not even once. Just stared until it whispered that soon army tanks would roll up Highland Avenue, that the reservoir would fill with bodies, that my name was on the list. I sat next to my mother on the couch, watching *Laugh-In.* Tiny Tim played his ukulele. "Sock it to me," he chirped in his loony falsetto, and was instantly drenched in a stream of water from offstage.

"What a nitwit," my mother quipped. She couldn't stop laughing.

My father read the newspaper. Darkness enveloped the house. He relayed that in secret pockets across America people had set fire to the American flag; boys were burning their draft cards. He knew exactly how many American soldiers had been killed in Vietnam.

"This is it," my father said clairvoyantly.

I didn't like when he talked like that. When the Vietcong and the NVA launched the Tet Offensive, my dad was the first to say that it was all over for the Americans; Vietnam would never ever surrender. I had seen on TV the famous footage of Colonel Nguyen Ngoc Loan, an American-backed police chief in Saigon, stick his pistol into the young Vietcong soldier's head and fire. The still photograph appeared on the front page of the *Press.* No one had seen anything like it before. I was eleven years old. The unarmed executed VC soldier wore a plaid shirt with a white T-shirt under it. His hands were tied behind him. He couldn't have been much older than me. He came up only to the shoulder of the man murdering him. Saigon burned in the background.

We all witnessed it. Again and again. The boy getting killed couldn't see it, but we saw it. 10,000 miles away and we saw it, but we would never know what he knew at the instant the bullet plowed into his brain. My mother turned away from it when it played on TV. She didn't like killing; she didn't really believe in the dirty things she said about black people or about my father. To her they were just words, as if words didn't matter, as if words couldn't put bullets in people the same as guns.

Suddenly the power went off and my mother screamed. Two seconds and it was back on. "Oh, my God, Oh, my God," she repeated. "They've cut the wires."

"The power's back, Rita. The wires obviously could not have been cut," said my dad.

"Dad," I said.

"It's okay, Fritz. The power went out for split second, and now it's back on. There's not a thing to worry about."

"Where's the gun, Travis?"

"Upstairs."

"Get the gun. It's probably time for you to get it. It's pitch-black out there."

My dad went upstairs and came back down with the gun. He held it by the muzzle as if he were about to hand it to someone. "I'm going out on the porch," he said, unlocking the front door. The second it opened we heard raised belligerent voices. One of them belonged to Alvin, our neighbor across the street. Then we heard his wife Millie's voice. Frantic, tearful. Alvin stood unsteadily on their porch. Their daughter, Olga, was there too. Alvin had Parkinson's, but he and Millie still walked the few blocks to Chookie's for lunch meat every day. It took them an hour, more. Often Alvin had to rest. Shaking, he'd stop and lean on Millie in the middle of the block until he could go on. My mother said she didn't want to live that long.

"Get out of here," Millie was shouting through her half-opened screen door.

"Jesus Christ," my mother intoned. "They're on Alvin's porch."

Alvin pointed a twitching finger at a man whose back was to us, but I couldn't hear what he was saying. The man was barking right in Alvin's face. Olga stood next to her father, shaking her fist at the man and yelling.

"I'm calling the police," Millie screeched.

The man bowled through Alvin and Olga, knocking Alvin over. The man slammed the storm door in Millie's face, and its huge glass panes shattered. Millie screamed, then started sobbing, and Olga jumped on the man, who was *goddamming* and *motherfucking* everything at the top of his voice. Glass fell and fell, as if every window in their house were breaking across the boards of the porch. Millie had disappeared, but we heard her crying. Alvin tried to pull himself up by the glider, but he flopped uncontrollably, falling back to the porch floor every time he reached his knees. Olga and the man punched at each other. He staggered each time he swung, as if drunk.

"Shoot that son of a bitch, Travis." Then my mother began screaming, "Shoot, shoot, Travis. Shoot him."

My father had turned the gun around in his hand. He held it against his thigh. Alvin and Millie's porch light was off. The street was black except for the solitary streetlamp. But you could still see that the man on the porch punching Olga was Chip, Olga's husband. There was bad blood between him and Alvin and Millie. We knew that much. There had been other scenes. Some of the neighbors had come out onto their porches. The men had guns.

"Shoot, Travis," my mother urged. "Shoot that black bastard."

My dad lifted the gun. Sirens looped in from all around us. Then a far off explosion. The power sparked off again. The streetlamp fizzed and died.

"Shoot, Travis. Goddam you, shoot."

My father started shooting. Like he was Rita Sweeney's killer. As if, all along, he had known what it would take to fill the space between us and what was waiting with enough fire to put the future in its grave.

FADING AWAY

The instant Fritz sees her at Keith Gentile's party it clicks. Claire Raffo. The pitiful little girl way back at Saints Peter and Paul school who sobbed herself sick every day over lunch, while the gorgeous Sister Hyacinth smiled and drilled her in lovely soprano to eat and banged the table with her yardstick. In all these years Claire has not crossed his mind, yet when he sees her now, the memory of those daily lunch room scenes ratchets through his head in a jagged narrative.

Usually more than willing to remain anonymous, to keep what he knows to himself, he is not in the habit of instigating conversation. But tonight he walks up to Claire Raffo, standing out on Keith's balcony, drinking wine from a coffee mug. A beautiful summer Saturday night. Music. Stars. Languor. The bravado of two pipes of opiated hash in the alley with Keith.

It's obvious she doesn't remember him, but she's friendly, and pretty in a soft, yet durable, way. Nothing like his mother and her cronies: hard, smart-mouthed women with dyed hair and dresses too short to flatter their lumpy legs. Fritz explains that he and Claire know each other. As he looks into her face, a wholly bemused, beatific face, he realizes that he's been watching her all night. A little like destiny. What are the odds of reconnecting this way? After all those years? Tonight this appeals to him: the romantic notion that perhaps there is an order to things, and that he and Claire have all along been situated together in its flow.

"That was a long time ago," Claire says. Her voice is a smoky whisper. It hangs in the air between them. She looks him dead in the eye, like there's nothing in the world that scares her.

Those days back in the school basement at lunch: they seem like a life that someone else lived, something he might have read about or dreamt. Claire's tiny, birdlike eyes the color of aluminum, threatening to drop onto the table. How terrified she was of Hyacinth, in her sleek black habit, coming down with the yardstick on the table next to Claire sitting there like the rest of them on the folding mortuary chairs with DeRosa stenciled on their backs. Her plaid uniform jumper hanging off her. Starved-looking, like one of the spindly black children on the mission stamps they collected money for at Christmas and Easter. Before her sat the white tablet of untouched bread. She would lay a hand upon it as if swearing an oath.

"Pick up your sandwich, Miss Raffo," Sister Hyacinth would say in a gentle, measured voice, barking the table with her stick, Claire starting out of her seat at each report. "Pick it up." Hammering again until the little girl started to cry. From the lap of her uniform skirt, she'd lift her other hand and with both hoist the sandwich to her mouth, and peck it, Hyacinth swooping in and out, pounding the table until Claire came apart, turquoise veins spiraling out of her papery skin, mouth clotted with meat and bread, tears and drool from her silently wailing mouth dripping from her chin.

"Swallow, Miss Raffo." The wood bamming down to punctuate each of Hyacinth's syllables, Claire, quivering, melting into the prismatic glass of the round, rose window that looked out on the playground. "It's a sin to waste when so many pagan stomachs go unfilled day after day."

Fritz and Claire stand on the balcony, looking out over the alley. Potholed asphalt; black chunks of rocky tar scored out of the roadbed by Pittsburgh winters; the distant, otherworldly lights of downtown. His hands, palms down, lie on the wrought iron balustrade. When he looks down, it's too much like the scaffold he scales every day for a pittance wage, a hod stacked with a hundred pounds of bricks on his shoulder, the blinding sun insisting he leap into it, the skinny planks beneath his work boots checked and splintering. Keith's little patch of peppers and tomatoes rush up at him, and he begins to fall. When he comes to, he is sitting on the balcony floor, Claire next to him, Keith and his girl Bonnie leaning down, a knot of people surrounding them. Claire's open hand rests against the middle of his back. He clutches the balusters.

"You okay, buddy?" Keith asks.

"Yeah, I'm alright."

"I'll get you some water," Bonnie offers.

"That hash," Keith says. "It's like acid."

"I'm okay."

Claire says nothing, her hand white against his blue work shirt. There's the music and the party, dancing, the smell of grass and hash, clink of bottles.

He takes the water from Bonnie and drinks half of it down.

"Thanks, Bon. I'm fine, you guys. Honest to God. I just got a little light-headed."

Claire doesn't move her hand, even when the others back away. She and Fritz sit silently side by side on the balcony.

He turns and looks at her. Pink bowed lips, but no lipstick. He knows that a seam has opened. "I'm okay," he says, and smiles, though he does not mean to.

"I know."

"I probably need to take a little walk."

"I probably need to come with you."

When she moves her hand from his back, as they get to their feet, he instantly feels its absence.

They walk to Tootie's for coffee. Cutting through the alley, they cross into a space, just before they emerge into Penn Avenue and the full thrum of light and traffic, where they turn to each other, as if the moment had been mapped out long ago in the basement of Saints Peter and Paul school—music pouring out of Keith's (*I should've stayed on the farm, I should've listened to my old man*)—and kiss.

Claire takes his arm as they walk the half block on Penn and enter the garish diner. No booths, just a counter. They take high stools and order coffee from Pam. Front teeth only, no molars, a bag of netted, concrete-colored hair, pencil behind her ear, a lime uniform trimmed with a white collar and short, white-cuffed sleeves. She sits in a chair behind the counter and works crosswords, every so often singing out, "You good, Fritzy?" And getting up, no matter Fritz's response, to top their cups. One other customer: a fat old black guy with a Pirates cap and a burgundy Banlon shirt, Chili and a milk shake. The place is cruddy in a homey way, the fluorescent tubes coated with dust, grimy bowling trophies shelved above the grill. What all-night's about.

Fritz wants to ask Claire what it was that kept her from eating her lunch all those years ago. Now that he's resurrected that picture, he can't erase it: like she's some bleeding icon, one of those leper kids waiting on Jesus in Catechism coloring books. It's the question that nagged him even then: *Just eat. Please. And then Hyacinth will shut her mouth and put that stick down.*

But instead he spills about his job working for his Uncle Pat's brick outfit as a hod carrier, how he has to climb scaffold, and it has him scared to death, that even going up and down stairs has him quivering. He has dreams about falling or the scaffold imploding. There's an omen sitting on his head like a black nimbus and he doesn't know what to do.

"Quit," Claire says.

"I can't."

"Why?"

"It's my uncle's company. My mother's brother. You know. I don't know. Disgrace."

"Death is worse than disgrace."

"I'm not sure I know the difference between the two. What am I gonna say: I'm scared?"

Claire holds his hand as he talks. He wonders how she has made this leap. From that petrified little girl, so immobilized by fear that she couldn't even chew, to this self-assured woman. She wears a gauzy white blouse that buttons to the neck and a red silk scarf. Nothing in her soft brown hair. Brown eyes. A bumpy bone in the middle of her aquiline nose that shines in the harsh light. Claire is good-looking in a way he can handle. Above all she seems even. Not like the other Italian girls he knows, not like his mother. Not that mouth, that streetwise swagger, the opera. His mother is crazy.

"Have you ever thought about talking to someone?" Claire asks.

"Like a psychiatrist?"

"A counselor."

"Same difference."

"Have you?"

"Not really. I'm too afraid to admit I'm afraid. If that makes any sense."

"At least you're honest about it."

"I'm not honest about anything."

He squeezes her hand; she leans from her stool and kisses him. The guy with the Pirates hat sleeps propped on his hand. Outside, the darkness breaks apart on Sunday morning.

Claire kisses him again and tells him, point-blank, that she's falling for him. Fritz, for the time being, refuses to consider what this means. Claire has entwined herself around him on the blue stool. Pam looks up from her crossword, nods to herself, and smiles, just those few slices of teeth in front. Fritz pulls Claire to him and hangs on a moment.

■

Claire is already in college. She left Peabody High School a year early, skipped her senior year, and enrolled at the University of Pittsburgh. She rented an apartment with money she's been saving for years babysitting and working at her family's landscaping business. She works now part time at the university's day care. She left home mainly to get away from her father, a squat, powerful, overprotective immigrant who slapped his wife and daughters in the name of old-world propriety. When he fell into a rage, he would break furniture and put his fists through walls. After Claire moved out, he disowned her, but she finds time when her father is gone to visit her mother and sisters.

"He's an animal," Claire says.

Fritz has seen Claire's father watering the Raffos' tiny lawn in the early evening, his thick, naked torso matted in dark hair, a black cigar hanging out of his mouth, his red pickup packed with lawn mowers and muddy tools parked at the curb.

Claire has a boyfriend named Allen Compton. Not really her boyfriend, she explains; she's finished with him, but he refuses to acknowledge that it's over. She was emphatic: told Allen that he turns her stomach, that he desperately needs help, that she never wants to lay eyes on him again. But Allen didn't want to hear about it. He went to her bookshelf and started tearing books in half. One by one, looking at her the entire time, smiling. She pleaded with him to stop, afraid to give him too much grief, afraid he'd hit her. He had tried to kill her cat once for jumping on the table while he was eating. Ripped a curtain rod off a window and chased the cat around her apartment. Ended up smashing her aquarium, the Siamese fighting fish thrashing rhythmically on the hardwood floor, slower and slower, in tandem, until they died. When she threatened to call the police, he yanked the phone out of the wall.

Fritz knows all about Compton. A little guy who lifts weights. You can see it in his jaw, the muscle like a bulging walnut as he habitually chews gum, the lifter's vein that pulses along his bicep like a garter snake. One of those guys who tries to dignify being a hood. Black leather jacket, black pants, black T-shirt, cleated pointy black shoes that tie on the side, slick black hair sprayed over his eyes. He drives a lime four-barrel 442, jacked up in the rear, with mags and a Hurst shift. The practiced sneer. He's an animal, the kind of guy, if you crossed him—and you wouldn't even know you had crossed him—it would be a curse.

He'd pick the time and place. Everything might be fine. For months. A year. And then there he is. You just finished a game of two-on-two in Dilworth school yard. Sitting on the school steps facing Moga Street, a dead-end stretch of asphalt that expires at the escarpment that falls into the Hollow, a hundred-foot drop to Negley Run Boulevard. Across the boulevard, at the pinnacle of the facing cliff, loom the Harriet Tubman projects, a cluster of blonde brick and chain-link high rises. You can see the projects from where you sit, drinking Fanta grape and smoking cigarettes, your gray T-shirt black with sweat. When up Moga Street grinds the 442, power-shifting, petulant as a wild horse, as Compton jerks it across Saint Marie Street toward the school yard. That half-smiling face above the dashboard, Maltese cross dangling from the rearview. You drop the pop can and run back into the school yard, but Compton brings the car up over the curb, up the first step, gears down. Rides that 442 all the way up the concrete steps into the school yard, the front bumper sparking off the lip of each stair.

Fritz clears this vision from his head. He has no business thinking about Compton. As far as he's concerned, there is no Compton.

Claire's bed is a mattress on the floor under a window. Surrounded by candles, and covered in a blue batik spread, white doves outlined with gold sequins swooping across it. Huge, gold silky pillows fringed with tassels. Painted on the ceiling above the bed in smoking red calligraphy is: "Out of the ash / I rise with my red hair / And I eat men like air." The lines are from a poem written by Sylvia Plath, not long before her suicide. Fritz has never heard of her, but those red words sometimes drip on him as he lies in bed with Claire. He doesn't know what they mean, but they unnerve him much like the inscrutable lines of Latin chant often do. He'd like to erase those hovering words. Claire has read a few of Sylvia's poems to him. He doesn't get them, but he knows enough to be scared. Claire shows him a picture of Sylvia. He finds her perfectly lovely, ideal, the soft, feminine looks of the woman he'd like to marry, not terribly unlike Claire, nothing feigned about the contentment, the utter peace, on her face, the snug cardigan about her shoulders, the long, girlish dark hair.

One vicious winter morning in London, Sylvia deposited in her little children's bedrooms toast and mugs of milk, sealed their doorjambs, then stuck her head in the oven and turned on the gas jets. Claire tells him these things as though she understands perfectly the doctrine of inevitability, as if there is a moral to this story so plain that she needn't explain. Fritz feels for a moment the frigidity of that London flat, the unfathomable will of the woman who buttered the warm bread and poured the milk. If he allows himself another moment of introspection he will see illuminated what Claire is trying to tell him. But winter is months away. It is a warm summer night, and he is, for the moment, blessedly safe.

Fritz reclines on the bed, leaning against the wall, drinking from a pint of J. W. Dant bourbon and smoking a cigarette. He feels the sky, through the window, hovering above him. He turns and gazes into the night and counts six gold stars. Billie Holliday, though he does not recognize her voice, sings from the phonograph. The cat sits just beyond the candles and stares at him.

Claire sweeps out of the kitchen, into the bathroom that opens off the bedroom, and switches on the light. She leaves the door open. Her back is to Fritz. She looks at herself in the large mirror above the sink. The doorway frames her. She kicks off her sandals, and drops her skirt to the floor. Her calves are skinny; she doesn't shave her legs. The hair is dark. She unbuttons her blouse. It falls from her shoulders, down her arms to the floor. Then the panties.

Fritz wants to get up and turn off the bedroom lamp, to be hidden, just Claire, as if incandescent, lighting the doorjamb. But he knows better than to move. Silently he brings his pack of Newports to his mouth, lips out a cigarette, and lights a match. Claire's face in the mirror. He cannot say for certain, but she is looking at him. She doesn't like him to smoke, but he can't help it right now. He lights the Newport and squashes the flame between his thumb and forefinger. Her bra is white and lacy, a tiny bow at the scooped cleavage. Smoke drifts between Fritz and Claire. She reaches behind her and undoes the bra. It slides off, and she is naked, no longer looking at Fritz, but at herself in the mirror as she deliberately brushes her short brown hair, then raises her arms and pins it atop her head. Under each arm is a nest of thick brown hair.

Astonished, Fritz sinks lower into the pillows, feels the bourbon sluicing through him. With a damp washcloth, Claire sponges her neck, behind her ears, her shoulders, the white plane above her breasts, beneath each arm. Lets her hair back down. And turns, for the spell of two long drags, fully illuminated, white as an urn, the punctuation of pubis and areolae. Flicks off the bathroom bulb, and walks, now sepia, into the dimly lit bedroom toward Fritz. She smiles. In her hand is a lighter. As she dips to each wick and lights it, she holds an arm across her breasts, surprisingly heavy, and she is suddenly older, Fritz suddenly younger. She snaps off the lamp. As much as anything, he is afraid, swaying on a plank four stories up, ringed by candlelight.

Claire calls him *Frederick*, his given name, not Fritz. Saint Frederick was bishop of Utrecht and was trained in piety and sacred learning among the clergy of the church. The insane empress, Judith, admonished by Frederick for her numerous immoralities, employed two assassins to kill Frederick, and on July 18, 838, he was stabbed to death. He took his last breath reciting Psalm 144: *I will praise the Lord in the land of the living.*

"How do you know?" Fritz asks Claire. He is named after his mother's father, Federico, a peasant cobbler born in the Napolitano village of Formicola. In America, he was called Fred. Fred the shoemaker. He died when his shop burned down, years before Fritz was born.

"I looked it up. Don't you think it's fascinating?"

"In a way."

"We'll have to do something special on July 18. It's your feast day."

She goes on to tell him that Saint Claire, her patron, a notorious virgin, renounced all her worldly goods in spite of her family's opposition. She received the penitential habit from the hand of Saint Francis of Assisi. Her feast is August 12.

Fritz holds her with one hand and smokes with the other. The candle flames are perfectly still. The cat lies at the foot of the bed. A pewter vase of purple zinnias on the table. A packed bookshelf, on top of which is a portrait of Guru Maharishi Mahesh, the mystic the Beatles ran off with, a red dot stamped on his forehead, a cone of incense ash in front of him on a brass saucer.

Claire's world enthralls Fritz: the bright, tidy apartment, its candlelight and books, scented soaps and incense, her self-assuredness and intellect. She knows what she wants and says it: *Kiss me. Put your hand right here. Hold still for a minute while I turn over.* Often she weeps as they make love. Everything about her strikes him as true and immaculate. He doesn't have to thrash through clutter, like at his house, simply to make it from his bed to the bathroom. Nor the clutter of his parents' lives, their messy pasts, the layers of falsehood and secrecy that seem to shade their every word, his mother's long bouts of silence, how his own life in light of them remains enigmatic, incomplete. With Claire, he feels like somebody, like he has a name more than *Fritz,* which sounds like a fuse blowing, a small hissing dysfunction. He likes that his patron is a fire-breathing martyr who spat in the eye of the harlot queen, Judith. Claire's world is the parallel universe he has glimpsed occasionally through the scrim of dream, and now, somehow, he has slipped into it.

But often it's a threatening world as well, every bit as foreign to him as his mother's omertà-riddled Italian blood, passed onto him, then muddled even further by his father's Black Irish ancestry. She shows him a book she's reading in her comparative literature class: *Psyche and Symbol,* by Carl Jung. On its cover is a blue, red, and yellow mandala with a bloodshot eye in its middle. It makes Fritz dizzy to look at it. Claire tells him that since she's been reading it, beautiful childhood dreams have returned to her—but terrible things too: doors and windows open and close of their own volition; sometimes she hears voices; nothing is as it seems.

Without opening the book, Fritz knows that nothing is as it seems, but he reads a bit from it just to satisfy Claire. Little of it makes sense. The writing is swollen and circular. Yet Jung's notion of the collective unconscious appeals to him: that humans at conception are inexplicably imprinted with a cast of characters, what Jung calls "mythological types." Like the people in East Liberty: the shadowgraph nuns and priests, the shunned tribal blacks, the haunted Italians, the fallen junky angels rotting down on the corner, and then wanderers like him—all of them lorded over by suicidal bridges and the gothic, pinched spars of Saints Peter and Paul church. The thought of it makes him laugh. He tells Claire that East Liberty, where they both grew up, is their collective unconscious.

"We're all a bunch of Jungians," he says, though he doesn't know exactly what he's talking about. But Claire thinks his observation funny, "Brilliant," she says. They smoke kief from a pink glass pipe that's shaped like a heart. Claire's father is the stout, hairy, Vesuvian-tempered, violent, Italian immigrant, landscape gardener archetype. He devours maidens between loaves of split Italian bread. Fritz's mother is the foul-mouthed, chain-smoking, bleached-blonde, black-browed Napolitano bitch archetype.

They laugh and laugh until Claire grows maudlin. She tells Fritz that she'll die if she doesn't escape East Liberty, leave Pittsburgh altogether. She'd like to transfer from Pitt to a university in Arizona or California. There's a holy man she's heard about in Kentucky. Maybe she'll go off and study with him. Fritz thinks about getting out, but he doesn't really want to leave Pittsburgh, or even the neighborhood. He is comforted by its terrain and predictability, its mythological types. He doesn't really want anything but to be left alone—but not by Claire. He squints his eyes and makes an attempt to see his life in terms of the future. Suddenly, as if one of those doors Claire had been talking about earlier has just swung open, the image of the scaffold, horizontal and vertical bars of steel rising out of sight, appears before him. Then Claire is laughing again, and it's clear that the kief and the wine have gone to her head.

On the job, Fritz eats lunch with Shotty Montesanto, one of the bricklayers he labors for. Shotty looks out for him: spotted him steel-toes and gloves, picks him up every morning, drops him off at the end of the day right in front of the house. Shotty's half crippled from going down on a scaffold years ago. He blames its collapse on Fritz's Uncle Pat. Every day Shotty figures out a way to bring it up. Fritz honors all of Shotty's kindness to him by suffering through his habitual replay of the accident. Shotty is another mythological type: the cussing, irascible bullshitter with a secret wound and heart of gold who fancies himself Rudolph Valentino. Slap a goat's ass on him and, with his goatee and widow's peak slicked up like horns, instant satyr.

Shotty is smoking and killing the second of the two or three beers he drinks every day at lunch. He and Fritz have five minutes before they hit the fiery hot part of the shift. Fritz stretches out on an empty mortar bag, his eyes closed, one hand behind his head; the other, with his cigarette, on his bare chest. Smoke glides through the glare fronting them; the sheer heat of the early August afternoon buckles everything.

A block truck rumbles through the site, huge bound squares of ten-inch concrete blocks chained to its bed. The driver waves at Fritz and Shotty, then drives through the blinding sun and crashes into the invisible town house that Pat's crew is bricking. The cab and driver disappear into the building, the back half of the truck tailing out through the wall. Some of the recently laid bricks have yet to set up, and like dominos they begin toppling from the town house; then the wall ties heave loose and an entire section whomps down over the truck bed. The gable splits off from the eaves; the last dozen courses of chimney brick let go, plummeting into huge plates of window glass loaded on a pickup parked next to the foundation. The roofers, clinging to their chicken strips, three stories up, belly down against the boiling tar paper as the entire building shimmies in the dull glowing stillness.

Then the scaffold on the building's lee side, where Fritz and Shotty sit, trips. The bucks score at their joints, and the scaffold begins to tip toward Shotty and Fritz. Two bricklayers, taking lunch up there on it, slide off like pucks; then the mortarboards and tools and all the planking tear loose, the steel bucks whining as they twist.

Shotty crabs up first, but his mangled, blood-starved legs fail him, and he scrapes away like an infant from the scaffold that is bending like a prehistoric bird toward him, until Fritz hoists him by his shirt and they clamber off.

No one moves, or even speaks. The entire site goes silent. Like *The Day the Earth Stood Still*, a palpable gear-grinding halt to everything, the prelude to the final disastrous crescendo. Fritz, on his knees with Shotty, peers up at the roofers stretched out on the quavering roof. He wants this to be a dream, like the ones Claire has told him about. A dream that stops, regardless of the dreamer's peril, the moment he wakes up.

"See," Shotty is saying, as if *see* is enough to capstone what just happened. *See*: synonymous with inevitability, with bad luck. Fritz knows what Shotty is saying, Shotty the prognosticator; he is warning Fritz: *You're next, my man.* As if to punctuate this, a convoy of screaming police cruisers, ambulances, and a township fire truck careen into the site. Workmen come out from their cover, accounting for themselves. Crews assemble. The fire truck veers dangerously against the dying building, then hydraulics its elevated platform to the roof. The marooned roofers inch into its protective cage and are lowered unharmed. One of the bricklayers who slid off the scaffold has a sprained ankle and lacerations, but that's all. No one is hurt.

The ruined building refuses to fall. Finally the driver of the block truck reappears through the front door of the town house. He wears the blameless, plain face of ignorance. Pat tears out of nowhere and punches him, then again and again, until the cops pull him off.

"See," Shotty says again.

Lady Day gutters on: "Strange Fruit." Her voice is like the gloomy cathedral light of an all-day rain: *blood on the leaves and blood at the root.* Fritz has no idea what exactly she's singing about, but he feels the suffering in it. It takes him back to 1959, the basement lunch room where Claire cowered daily.

Claire confesses that she did not hate Hyacinth at all, but blames herself.

"Why?" Fritz asks. "You were just a little kid."

"She was so beautiful. I wanted to be like her. I wanted to be a Sister. At home, I'd go to my room and drape myself with my bed sheet, pin a pillowcase to my head, and spin out rosary after rosary. I dreamed of martyrdom, going down in a snarl of wild dogs, the headsman poised above me as I refused to denounce the Son of Man, scrawling with a bloody finger a crude fish in the dust of the arena, my last breath triumphant, whispering 'dark sayings of old.'"

Fritz smiles. "Where do you get all this?"

"It's from a poem I'm writing."

"I wanted to kill Hyacinth for what she did to you."

"Didn't you think she was beautiful?"

"I hated her even more for that."

"Were you ever in love with her?"

"I was afraid of her."

Fritz suddenly remembers the day Hyacinth called upon him to read and he had lost his place. She summoned him to the front of the class and commanded him to read. She hovered behind him, beneath the cross of hard-luck Jesus, executed a mere three years into His public life, her arms at right angles, the habit sleeves swooping like blackbird pinions. Gleaming from the pristine pages splayed out in his hands were Mother, Father, Dick and Jane, Spot and Puff. They gazed up at him querulously as he tried to say their names and describe their perfect pastel kingdom. But the vowels and consonants roiled like chromosomes. He felt faint, not just that he would lose consciousness, but pass into fire. Heat flared off Hyacinth. He smelled brimstone. All he could do was stutter as the other children laughed. What brought him to was Hyacinth angrily rapping the blackboard, behind which he imagined purgatory: trapped, smoldering children, like him, who had lost their places.

Sister Hyacinth led him to the principal's office and the school's lone telephone. He was to call home and explain to his mother how he had not been paying attention. He dialed Emerson 1-8104 again and again. Each time there was no answer. It was noon. He knew that his parents were home, in all likelihood unclothed, still too drugged by the blessed forgetfulness of something not quite sleep to remember they had a son.

The phone rang and rang as he looked out the principal's window and saw the men the sisters called Negroes passing a jug of Tokay, and two coupling dogs dancing on six legs up the middle of Flavel Street. He can still hear that empty, ceaseless ring of solitude.

Fritz lights another cigarette. Claire takes it out of his mouth and stubs it out in the ashtray.

"Don't smoke."

"Okay."

"Stay here tonight."

"I shouldn't. I really can't. My mother will worry." This is bullshit and he knows it.

"Stay."

It is not honor, it is not that Fritz does not love her, but the fear that she will devour him, that prompts his hesitance. That old face of the little girl trapped with Hyacinth in the cellar, the face that kisses him now, and says, "Stay. Stay, *Frederick*," more than once, its mouth a hunger. That little girl. He wishes he could go back for her.

"I want you to stay." She rolls on top of him, raises up on her forearms and kisses him. Her pale breasts swag against his chest, dark like the rest of him from laboring summer-long in the sun.

There is a furious knocking at Claire's front door.

"That's Allen," she says, suddenly a wreck, jumping up, ripping the sheet off the bed and wrapping it around herself.

Fritz rolls off the bed and sits on the floor, tugging on his pants.

"Just wait right here," Claire cautions. She hurries across the room and down the flight of stairs to the front door.

Fritz walks to the kitchen and pulls a long, serrated bread knife from one of the drawers. He stands at the top of the stairs, just out of sight, and tries to make out the conversation between Claire and Compton. Their voices wend up to him like another language, urgent, strained. He can't stop his left leg from shaking. He's heard that Compton has a gun. What will he do if Compton marches up the stairs? The front door slams, and a moment later comes the sound of skidding mags and the four-barrel kicking in. Claire walks tiredly up the stairs. "He's gone," she says. "Please stay."

Whenever Fritz is with Claire, he is aware of the phantom presence of Compton, that he might out of nowhere hurtle into sight, and finally they'll be face to face. He's been keeping regular company with Claire, spending the night at her apartment two or three nights a week. On those nights in particular he is especially afraid that Compton will again present himself, and that Claire will not dissuade him from entering.

When Claire talks about Compton or her father, Fritz simply listens, nodding occasionally. Sometimes he'll hold her hand or put his arm around her, but the indisputable presence of these two violent males in her life makes him fretful.

Fritz has never been a fighter, but he determines to train for what he senses is his inescapable showdown with Compton. All summer he has carried hods of brick and mortar under a brutal sun. He is in the best physical shape since his two years as a high school wrestler. He is not large, but strong and lithe, and certainly as big as Compton.

Each day when he gets home from the job, he tugs off his heavy work boots, slips into his tennis shoes, and runs up to Highland Park, then around and around the reservoir. He doesn't even bother exchanging his mortar-caked pants for shorts. He just wants to get on the road, feel his legs taking him over the pavement, his feet slapping time, like he's gaining ground on the mysterious earth, preparing for Compton or Mr. Raffo, for his ultimate confrontation with fate. He does push-ups and sit-ups, little muscle-building routines with bricks instead of weights.

"What's going on with you, Fritzy?" his mother asks one late afternoon, as she and Fritz's father are about to depart for work.

Fritz looks up from the living room floor where he is doing sit-ups. His mother slips her black dress over her head, then snaps her hands to her hips and looks intently down upon him. She has not yet applied her makeup, and her face has an unguarded softness. Fritz is tempted to tell her about Claire and Compton and the scaffold, that he's scared. She doesn't look at him this way often, as if she is capable at that moment of accepting anything he might confess, and then offering the precise comfort he desperately needs.

"Nothing," he answers.

"Don't gimme that," she says. "You don't come home at nights. Now all this running and the exercises. What the hell's going on?"

"Nothing. I'm just running."

"After you work all day in the hot sun? You're shacking up somewhere too."

"What are you talking about?"

"Hey, Fritz. I know what's what. Okay?"

Fritz gets off the floor. "Okay, Mom. Thanks for the concern. I feel a lot better now."

"Don't get smart with me. You're going to get yourself into a peck of trouble, boy. Who is this little tramp you're sneaking around with?"

"Like you'd know whether I was home or not."

"What's that supposed to mean?" Fritz's mother lights a cigarette. She lifts her face to the ceiling and spits out a long funnel of smoke.

"And you know what else?" asks Fritz, pointing a finger at her, knowing the gesture will infuriate her, that after this plays out she probably won't speak to his father and him for who knows how long.

"What else?" she demands, taking a step closer to Fritz.

"Cut it out, Rita," his father shouts from the kitchen.

"Kiss my ass, Travis," she shouts back. "I want to know what else."

"You know what else," Fritz says.

His father appears in the doorway, knotting a maroon bow tie.

"Yeah, here's what else." She flicks the lit cigarette to the carpet, then grabs from an end table a tall, milk glass statue of the Madonna. Mary and the Christ-child smash on the wall behind Fritz.

Travis walks into the room and smiles. The way Fritz has seen him smile on his way into a funeral home. He steps on his wife's cigarette. "That was very Italian, Rita."

When Fritz runs, he feels like he is doing something, not simply waiting around for inevitable disaster, but training. Up Highland Avenue and around the reservoir, ten, fifteen revolutions, logging miles along the same path, revisiting the same thoughts—*Compton, Claire, the scaffold, old man Raffo*—his flayed Converse tennis shoes flattening with every stride.

He often ends his runs at Claire's, sitting on her kitchen floor, sweat ringing from him, listening to John Coltrane blow a feverish gale of sorrow through his sax, waiting for his breath to return so he can smoke a cigarette, for the cup of tea Claire has given him to cool. Despite the heat, her skin looks cool, and her flimsy purple dress blows in the open window breeze. The wind is hot. She molts out of her dress. She wants him to leave Pittsburgh with her. Where, she doesn't know. *Out West.*

"I want to get out of here, Frederick."

Why not? he thinks. The scaffold, his parents, Compton: leave it all behind. Forget about it. But his imagination is hemmed in by Pittsburgh, by East Liberty. He thinks *out West*, and the only thing that registers is blonde desert and jagged ochre buttes. He attempts to envision himself in this lonely, unrelieved expanse, but he is already lost.

He listens to Claire and nods. New Mexico: she's read about it. Or the Yucatán. Or British Columbia. A commune. The Peace Corps. Maybe to a monastery.

"A monastery?" Fritz asks. He has her up against him, his sweat on her shimmering in the sun.

"For sanctuary," she says. "And commitment. Coarse robes. The undefiled word of God."

Fritz doesn't know how to respond. At times he worries that Claire is about to crack. He is sure he hears Compton's souped-up car idling outside, like a force field imprisoning Claire that only he can shatter. He just wants to get it over with.

Fritz buys real running shoes. Twenty-two bucks for a pair of gold Kangaroo-skinned Adidas. He runs eight, ten miles a day, often more. Begins to conceive of himself as someone blessed with unlimited endurance, like his father. A man who can take it and take it. As he runs he views himself with crystalline objectivity: one foot after another, north and south, respiration even, his heart rhythmic, untroubled. He never wants to stop.

Claire cooks supper. They sit in her kitchen and eat like a married couple. She reads poetry to him, and they drive to the university in Claire's navy Corolla to see free foreign films. They sleep in her bed and make love. He looks down at the world from the scaffold and sees Shotty gazing up at him. Through his every waking moment Compton's 442 idles like the Minotaur.

One night they are awakened by the sound of pulverized glass. Crash after crash. Then the 442 screeching up the street. Fritz gets to the window first and sees, in the apron of light cast by the streetlight, the pool of glass Claire's car sits in. Every window smashed, the headlights and taillights. Lights sprinkle on in a few of the houses along the street.

Sometimes when Fritz is running up the park he spots Mr. Raffo in his bright red truck, his big hairy arm, a cigar at the end of it, hanging out the window. When this happens, he tacks on an extra few miles, adding to his endurance. Lately he's come to think of Mr. Raffo and Compton as the same person, a mutated mythological creature: *animale.* He suddenly realizes that endurance is a curse. Yes, his father has endurance, but it is his mother's operatic blaze that influences the world, her willingness to torch everything on a whim: vendetta, caprice. He begins to tire. Instead of getting stronger, he is getting weaker, skinnier and skinnier. He barely eats. He feels himself fading away.

Claire tells Fritz, as he holds her in the flickering candlelight, that Compton once forced a pistol muzzle into her mouth. She laughs as she tells him, but Fritz has come to recognize that laugh as powerlessness. What people of epic endurance possess. They only know how to suffer. Not to hit back. Then he hears himself laugh too. It finally occurs to him that he has been training not to fight, but to flee. He contemplates guns and knives, dynamite, fire. Not fighting, but murdering the *animale.*

"I know this sounds crazy, but I'd still like to become a nun."

"After what that witch, Hyacinth, did to you?"

"I still love God, the romance and poetry of the spirit."

Fritz does not know what this means. He lights a cigarette and sees that it irritates Claire. She turns away to sip a glass of water. A shard of light from the streetlamp catches her shoulder, the crescent scar from the first time Compton bit her.

"Did you know that Saint Hyacinth was a man?" Claire asks. "He was scourged for the faith and martyred in Rome in the year 260. His feast is September 11."

Maybe, more than anything, it was the impotent rage of childhood Fritz had felt back then. Hyacinth's yardstick, as if it were chopping inside him: *crack, crack, crack.* Her pretty, melodic voice: *Eat, Miss Raffo. For the little breechclouted starvelings of Fiji, the baby lepers of Burma . . .*

He'd been just a tiny boy, but he had perfectly envisioned killing Hyacinth: He'd warn her, tell her to lay off Claire, give her every chance to repent as it says in the gospels, then ride in, the Angel of Love, with his poison kiss.

"I'd like to be martyred," Claire says.

"Don't talk like that."

"Wouldn't you like to be a saint?"

"No. That's all bullshit. Don't even say it."

"'Don't even say it ?' You're so superstitious, Frederick."

"I'm not Frederick, Claire. I'm Fritz. Just Fritz."

"No one is just Fritz. I wish you wouldn't smoke."

Fritz gets out of bed and walks to the window, blows smoke through the screen, stares at the red glowing tip reflected in the lifted pane as he takes another long drag. Across the street from Claire's apartment is Compton's 442.

"Why the fuck didn't you eat your lunch, Claire?"

When Claire doesn't answer, Fritz turns back toward her. She is sitting up, the sheet pulled to her waist, her quaint, cropped face quizzical, hair cut in a veil at her nape, enormous silvery eyes crowning out of her sockets. The only thing to distinguish her from that little girl left in the cellar in 1959 are her uncovered breasts, heavy, iconographically carnal, nearly a desecration the way they hang in the shadows like halves of the same jilted moon.

As if he were glass, she looks through him at the night beyond her window. "I was trying to fade away," she says. What Fritz, all along, has not figured out how to do.

Finished with their lunches, the other children, Fritz included, used to leave her, whimpering, choking on the food she could not swallow, abandoned to Sister Hyacinth. Up the long, marble stairs, down the hall to the lavatory, then out to the school yard for recess, Fritz heard the echo of Hyacinth's stick, then finally the silence of Miss Raffo as she faded away. He hears Hyacinth even now, but it's a car door slamming. Compton's. Fritz turns to the window and watches him, black-clad and hunched, traverse the street toward Claire's front door.

Maybe Fritz wheels too abruptly back to Claire. Perhaps it's that the second-storey window he's perched at, looking down, becomes the scaffold, and he realizes suddenly that he is naked, that his cigarette has burned out in his knuckles. Whatever it is, he staggers, and a wash of panic breaks over him. He begins to sweat. Claire is already on her feet, completely naked, headed as if sleepwalking toward the stairs leading down to the door.

"Claire," he calls, but she doesn't turn.

He hears the front door kicked open, Compton's cleats on the wooden stairs.

Fritz once saw Compton fight a black kid from the projects down the Hollow, along Negley Run. Blacks on one side of the boulevard, whites on the other. The black kid's name was Patterson. Tall, handsome, no shirt, big defined pecs and biceps, and a pair of green work trousers. Compton, a good head shorter, in all black, the twisted mouth and Marlboro, labyrinth of gleaming black brittle hair, even the oily leather jacket in June. Sweat rolled out of Patterson. A few yards away, under the Hoeveler Street Bridge, a stinking dead dog lay ballooned on the shoulder. Patterson and Compton sparred a bit, open-handed jabs and jukes.

Patterson grabbed Compton and lifted him. Like Atlas. Beautiful in the early summer green of the Hollow. Muscles washed in sweat. Sunlight. Compton, going up and up, cradled in those black arms, the throng of white kids jeering, picking from the ground things to throw. The blacks skirting the curbs for rocks, screaming for Patterson to kill Compton. Crack him in half on the boulevard.

But Compton, still in Patterson's arms, wrenched him in a headlock, popped him three quick in the face, then leered in and bit him on the cheek. Patterson dropped him and screamed. The black kids started with the rocks, then the whites; then more blacks bounding down the cliff from the projects. By then Compton had gone *animale*, punching Patterson over and over, moving in and out with demon speed until Patterson's face was a bloody shroud. He fell to the ground and wept, yet Compton, in a hail of rocks glancing off his black leather, continued to pound him. Patterson rolled over on his stomach, wrapped his hands around his head. Compton sat his back like a saddle horse, pried his hands away, and punched him in the head, dipped in and bit Patterson's fingers. Took his time with the punches. Never stopped. Compton with the brute, cockstrong smile. Mythological type: fallen angel with nine lives. The Reaper.

"Claire," Fritz calls again.

But she has faded away.

BOMB BOULEVARD

I wake up between my parents in a booth in Finnegan's, an all-night diner on Baum Boulevard. I think it's *Bomb* Boulevard, though, because Khrushchev says he will bury us; any day the bomb will drop.

Finnegan's is a silver rusting box like a caboose, surrounded by used car lots strung with beaming lightbulbs on wires, prices waxed in big soapy numbers across the windshields. Across the street is Baddour's, neon minarets scrawling up the sides of the doorjamb, a Lebanese restaurant where my parents eat kibbe. Raw lamb. Next to Baddour's looms a once fancy funeral home, now falling apart, called Van Landingham's. But in the distancing half-light of 2:30 A.M., it looks like *Gone with the Wind*, and there's a fountain with baby angels coughing water in its big front yard.

My mother never fails to remark when we're in Finnegan's that she wants to be laid out at Van Landingham's. Then she elbows my dad and says, "Did you hear me, Travis?" to which he responds, "Yes, Rita," or "Will do." Two black guys linger on the sidewalk smoking cigarettes after last call at Maxine Benko's Lounge, on the other side of Van Landingham's. They're telling a big story with their hands, and laughing. Fancy short-sleeved shirts and banded straw fedoras.

Cuss, a guy who waits tables with my dad at the Park Schenley, slumps across from us in the same booth. He and my dad are still in their white shirts and maroon vests, but they've stripped off their bow ties. Cuss whips out a silver flask every now and then and drips whiskey into everyone's coffee. He never stops talking, and he has a sneezy, nervous laugh—like he's going to swallow his lips.

"How do you keep flies out of the kitchen?" Cuss asks. My parents and Cuss go so far back, as kids in East Liberty, that it's like they're stuck with him. When no one answers, Cuss blurts, "Shit in the living room." Then he snorts like a Chinese pug. My dad just smiles at him, like he's embarrassed because I'm here, and without saying anything to each other, we both know Cuss is a real schmoe.

"You're a jagoff, Cuss," my mother says, dry as wine vinegar.

"I like a broad who speaks her mind," Cuss quips. "I like any broad at all." Then the laugh, like he doesn't even know he's doing it.

I'm in my pajamas. Bright red flannel with black fighter jets, even though it's mid-July. I don't even know how I got here.

"That's where I want to be laid out," my mother says, flicking her head toward Van Landingham's towering white columns.

"Good choice, Rita," my dad replies right away. He's stretched out, his feet up on the booth next to Cuss. Cigarette smoke trickles out of his nostrils, and he's smiling. Behind the counter, where the Greek guy who owns the place frantically cooks, a radio broadcasts the ball game, a mere three blocks away at Forbes Field, where the Pirates bat in the fifteenth inning of the second game of a rain-delayed twi-nighter against Sandy Koufax, the greatest pitcher of the twentieth century. Above Van Landingham's cupola sprays the eerie light from the Field. Like the epicenter of something unimaginable: the radiant last moments of the Second Coming.

"Extra innings," my dad says, smiling like crazy. Baseball's the only sport he really likes, because it's slow, contemplative. You can look away, think of other things. With it comes a kind of silence. You can barely hear the game. Finnegan's is packed: teenagers; restaurant people like my parents and Cuss, just off work; sweethearts; derelicts; lungers near homicidal from eating shit and grease, too much booze and nicotine, coffee kickback.

"The way to do it is pay ahead," Cuss says.

"Huh?" asks my mother.

"The funeral bill. You pay ahead, you know, before you croak. They lock you into a fixed rate, like a mortgage, and you make monthly payments: today's price for tomorrow's funeral. Everything. I mean embalming, casket, hearse, flowers, cemetery, down to the limo for the aggrieved loved ones left to endure in your tragic absence. You save a bundle. Who knows what it'll cost to get planted in forty, fifty years. Fifteen grand, I'll bet."

My dad is laughing and shaking his head. "So every month you pay the tab for your funeral?"

My mother has been studying Cuss. She puts her arm around me. I look into her big round golden earrings, like Roman battle shields, at my distorted reflection: my big head and spidery body, those jets taking off on their final mission.

"Yep." Cuss taps his temple with a finger. "Thinking ahead." Then he breaks into his blubbering, lip-sucking laugh, his forehead puckering like silly putty. "But," he appends through his snurgling, "you only save money if you live a long time—which is my plan."

"I'm not going to live a long time," my mother says. She seems to know that the world is about to end. It must be this dwindling that accelerates her appetites: one cigarette after another; dribble after dribble from Cuss's flask; her teased silo of calico hair elevating her, even seated, above my father; the carnal torque of her breasts launching through her lavender dress.

"You never know, Rita. You'd be wise to consider the future," Cuss advises.

"Piss on the future."

"Rita is naturally pessimistic," my dad says. "She has a death wish."

She turns on my father, then whispers, her lips against his ear. It might have been *fuck you* or *bastard.* Yet he smiles all the more, and they kiss savagely for an instant, leaving my dad's lips daubed in her purple lipstick. Now they'll fight. She is getting ready to lay into my father when the Greek rushes over to our booth. White apron over a T-shirt, arms crawling with black hair, and a soda jerk hat. His black eyes sit way back in his cave-like sockets. Banana cream pie for Cuss, pancakes for me, and he tops everyone's coffee.

The pancakes are beautiful. They look almost forbidden, taboo, as if I shouldn't look at them, the little scalloped ball of butter melting, along with the syrup, in uniform rivulets down over the golden edges. Exactly like the unapproachable glory of an Aunt Jemima commercial. It is 1963, and Khrushchev, his gleaming head like those lynched car lot lightbulbs, plots to gouge a hole so deep and wide that we will all fit into it.

The black guys cross the street, walk in the diner, and remove their hats. They're much, much older than I thought, and identical. Twins. Alabaster hair, parchment skin black as Good Friday. They could be messengers or priests. From Africa. Like they might have bad news, and it's too late. One of them weaves as he makes for a stool at the counter.

"You hear about the air-conditioned whorehouse?" Cuss blurts through a mouthful of pie. White cream coats his thick lips. I have no idea what he's talking about, but I know it's the beginning of a joke.

"Pour some more whiskey in this cup, you idiot," my mother commands.

Cuss slips the flask out of his vest and drops a stream into my mother's coffee, then my dad's.

"You've heard it before?" Cuss asks.

"Yeah, we've heard it before," my dad answers. He's trying to listen to the game, but suddenly Forbes Field's lights go out—no one else seems to notice—and there is just the memory of the lights, the strange afterglow mantling the vaporized field. Across the sky swatches the illuminated absence of what once was, then a sizzling black emptiness.

Cuss starts laughing, his mouth filled with the whipped pie, and still he's shoveling, laughing big, hyperventilating, phlegmy sighs like he'll choke, his head launched back, his Adam's apple pogoing up and down the pipes of his throat, where my mother, who has taken up her fork, will stab him just to get him to clam up.

"Get your feet down off there," the Greek yells, loud enough to be heard above all the rebop.

Everyone in the diner shuts up and looks at him.

"You," pointing at our booth. At my dad—I guess everyone in the place figures this out at the same time—because he's resting his feet on the booth seat across from him.

We gape at the Greek for a moment. Finnegan's is a dive, a plane about to crash, filthy poems and pictures all over its putrid bathroom. Not the Park Schenley, where people show up like they're somebodies and the maître d' wears a tuxedo.

My dad slips his feet off the browning yellow vinyl and puts them on the floor underneath the table. The Greek brother hurries back behind the counter. The rhythm of Finnegan's returns, but the snuffed light does not return. The black guys stare at our booth, looking so much alike, so unbelievably old, they must be, after all, angels.

My mother still clutches her fork, glowering at the Greek like she's going to get up and go after him. Then she looks at my dad, drinking his coffee as if nothing's happened—though he's hoping my mother won't make an issue of it. He's already traveled past this moment: what would have been humiliation to most men, to him is simply fact, and he doesn't give a damn about it.

He just wants my mother to stay put, to not get out of the booth with that fork in her hand.

She sneers at the side of my father's face; you can see that he feels it. He knows what's coming, and he can't help but smile. If somebody promised to pay him a million bucks if he got what's about to happen right, he'd describe it word for word, syllable for syllable, and he'd take home a million. My dad would be a millionaire because he knows my mother like a book. A book he's read over and over. And my mother: she'd tell him he can keep his million, shove it up his ass, she doesn't want a goddam red cent of it. He can take it with him to Miami Beach or Havana or wherever dreamers like him end up. He can go to hell.

"Punch his face in, Travis," my mother whispers to my dad's jawbone, and he smiles all the more. "If you love me, go after him. Kick his ass."

She spikes her white patent leather go-gos up on the booth in the grooves still there from my father's shoes. "Hey asshole," she screams at the Greek, the fork pointed toward his dark, stubbly face. "Tell me to put my feet down."

Silence again falls over Finnegan's. Cuss's mouth hangs open. The black angels rise.

The pancakes are divine, but I feel them turning to smoke inside me.

DECORATION DAY

My mother is stationed at the kitchen table when I come downstairs at six. Stone sober, coffee in one hand, a Chesterfield in the other, she wears a pale green velour robe, not a stitch under it, with a black cigarette scar smoldered into the left lapel. To my obviously surprised look, she parries: "Is it okay I'm up? Is it alright with you that I couldn't sleep and thought I'm come down and help get you off to work?"

I tell her it's fine with me. But something's up. She and my father, because they never get home from work until three, even four in the morning, never get out of bed until noon, often later. I have no clear memory of either of them ever seeing me off to school when I was a kid unless they had stayed up all night.

I sit across from her, pour a bowl of Cheerios, load it with sugar and milk, and keep an eye on her as I eat. She gazes out the window, a strip of sunlight boring into her forehead. What's left of her makeup shadows her face like jail bars. Her bleached hair sprays the wall behind her. The room gets brighter and brighter by the second. The last few days of May. You can almost feel the green rising, the birds singing their brains out.

"It's a nice day," she declares.

I've never heard her say such a thing, so I hesitate before answering, as if my response is somehow crucial to the way the rest of our lives will go.

Finally I agree. She smiles and says, "Today's my birthday."

I realize that indeed today is her birthday. My first impulse is to dispute this fact. Perhaps, because of my shame at having forgotten her birthday, I can convince her that she was not born on this date at all and be granted a reprieve: one more morning to rise up out of bed and go to her with a gift and loving wishes for long life. But it is not in my power to repair this breach. It is a thing that has happened, and now it sits there on the table like a ruined meal. It joins the trove of unredressed hurt that sustains my mother. Like a dead thing, it can't be called back to life.

"Happy birthday," I say, lean across the table and kiss her on the cheek.

She twists her smirk into me. "Thanks. But you didn't remember. You forgot."

"I didn't forget. I knew."

"You're a goddam liar. Just like your father."

She's right. I am a liar, but my father, a student of futility, isn't. For him, lying presents no moral dilemma. The truth is simply too much trouble. He's upstairs, sleeping, blessedly unaware of the shit storm brewing a mere ten feet beneath him.

"Do you remember the picnics we used to go on?" she asks.

I don't know where she's going with this. Some kind of setup, a little tunnel she'll lure me into, then spring an entire battalion of unimaginable recriminations. I brace and keep my eyes in the general vicinity of her face, not on her eyes because that would be a mistake, like looking certain breeds of dog in the eye. When my mother is mad, the seared, sharpened points of her fine brown eyes are too much for me. I fix on her neck, which is still pretty in a girlish, unguarded way, a part of my mother's body, like her still soft, smooth hands, that has held out against anger and disappointment. When I chance to glance up, however, I see that her eyes have in them no more than the color of a sidewalk after rain.

She pushes her cigarette pack to me, and whispers, "Go ahead and have one." She doesn't like me to smoke. "Go ahead." She cracks open the chrome Zippo and revs up a flame.

I slide a cigarette to my lips and she lights it. For half a minute we sit there together and fill our little brightening kitchen with pearly clouds of smoke. She's thinking about the picnics, she tells me, because today is her birthday, May 30, Decoration Day, and for a stretch of time when I was little—how long I couldn't say—every year on this day, my mother's entire family, in a procession of big '50s automobiles, motored out to North Park to picnic.

"Talk to me about the picnics, Fritzy. Tell me what you remember."

My mother is inventive. She knows I've forgotten that today is her birthday, and her gift to herself is to punish me for this epic lapse, to punish my father for it as well, which is why she got up so early. I'll bet she never went to bed. The night probably ended with the two of them sitting in exactly this same spot, my father trying for a while to reason with her. *Rita, I'm sorry as hell I forgot about your birthday. Let's just walk upstairs to bed. Me and you, Rita. Like nothing happened. You lead me up in case with this shitty memory I lose my way. Like I'm not the world's biggest cad, just a fool for you, Rita. A forgetful fool. C'mon, Rita. Rita. Jesus Christ. Rita. Happy birthday, Rita. You know . . .*

Realizing he was entreating stone, he would have then stubbed out his cigarette in the ashtray, shot her that wry smile, and walked out of the room and upstairs to bed. Then she stayed up to ambush me. Before my father could warn me. She didn't want either of us to remind the other about her birthday and cheat her out of a reason to be hurt and pissed.

"Tell me what you remember, Fritzy." Like an ultimatum, my penance is to tell her a story. I don't have long. Shotty, a bricklayer on my crew who rides me to work every day, will blow his horn for me at 6:30 down to the second hand. Before *good morning*, he'll impress upon me what a tight-ass jagoff my Uncle Pat is for making us work holidays and no overtime.

I sit in the soft backseat of one of my uncle's cars, my hand out the window, a toy flag fluttering at the end of it in the highway wind. My blonde cousins, Pat's kids, with their determined faces, look straight ahead, through the windshield, at the future rushing beneath the car in the opposite direction. My mother, up front in the middle between her brother Pat, at the wheel, and his beautiful wife, spins the quick story about a little boy she knew who dangled his arm out a car window and had it clipped off by a telephone pole. I see the boy's arm clatter to the roadbed and tuck mine back inside the car. It is so early in the morning that the cars have their headlights on. The sun waits another minute or so before leaking its yellow blood across the horizon.

At the park we commandeer a pavilion. The cars are unloaded. Red gingham-covered bushel-baskets filled with rigatoni, eggplant, and fried chicken, hotdogs, hamburgers. Square steel coolers of Iron City beer and Tom Tucker pop. The picnic tables are covered with the gingham tablecloths. Grills fired up. Poker. A portable radio keyed to KDKA. The hazy last bit of spring coats the grass, the foggy trees coming to life in the sun, mist rolling off the lake in billowing white shrouds.

The dead take their places in the hammocks and chaise lounges; they sidle up to the poker table. I shut my eyes, open them again, and still the dead moon about, content to watch the business of the living: the towels tucked in the grass, badminton nets hung, bocce balls deployed. A few of them root through the baskets for pepperoni and bread, the whiskey the men will begin drinking, chasing it with Iron City, as soon as the sun crests the trees.

Despite the fact that today is my mother's birthday, that today is a legal holiday set aside for fallen comrades, no work going on anywhere, even the restaurants closed; that this gathering of my mother's family will adjourn only once it is pitch dark, with a cake of blazing candles, the family ringing the pavilion in song to my mother—my mother who will tell them all to lay off, what the hell does she care about a cake and a birthday, the hell with that, please, it's just another day; my mother who must deny that there is anything about which she really cares—despite all this, my father is at home. And so, for a day—with my mother prowling about in her tight bathing suit, cigarettes, and that exaggerated bravado when she's around Pat, the shots, the beers, the coarse language and crazy chances she takes off the diving board—I am an orphan.

I don't know if I miss my dad, but I feel incomplete. Like people are whispering behind their hands about me. A boy destined to accept handouts. A mutt. No future. A boy without even sufficient anger to plot revenge. Not like Pat's kids with their golden mother and legacy of gentrified propriety. I don't know what it is I want, but I know I am uncomfortable, and crave my mother's touch, the withering love she parses out like morphine.

The dead reach toward me with cookies through the cottony sphere that separates us. I have trouble distinguishing between the dead and the living. I recognize, however, my grandfather, Federico Schiaretta, for the dead man he is. My namesake, a shoemaker, he burned to death in 1942 when his shop on Station Street caught fire. My mother was nine years old. Smoke leaks out of him when he tries to smile at me. Like my grandfather, the other dead wear the garments of requiem, dusted with the earth they must rest in.

Among the living, there are strangers as well: uncles, aunts, and cousins I cannot remember, the family my mother has hidden me from. There have been among her and her family secrets and vendettas. For long periods they splinter and refuse to speak. Most of all, there is my father, the *americano,* the Irish, whom she had to marry because of me. There is the *infamia* of my mother. And there is Pat, who is afraid of nothing. He knows the dead and accounts for them the way he might a yard of concrete or a pallet of bricks. Some day I will labor for him, toting the deadweight hod of mortar and brick, stepping through the sky on faulty planks. The living mingle unwittingly with the dead as if they can't see them, everyone but my grandmother, my mother's mother, whom everyone treats with a practiced distant decorum. She is a gypsy who reckons the dead and does not fear them.

What I want most is to swim in the immense North Park pool, which opens every year, like the other pools across the city, on Decoration Day. The women and girls crowd into the cars. They drape towels across the windows and change into their bathing suits. The men, however, change in the pool's public bathhouse. My mother entrusts me to Pat and my other uncles, Pete and Lawrence. Their sons, all older than me, come along too. They pay no attention to me. Not unfriendly; they just don't know me. My uncles are tall men with hairy, knotted brown arms and kinky hair. I have no recollection of Pete and Lawrence, but Pat, whom my mother adores and despises by turns, but never wholly detaches herself from, has been a shadow, like my grandmother, all along in my life. Pat and Rita: their relationship is like a cigarette left in an ashtray. No one puffs it; it just smokes. Pat and my father do not like each other.

At the door of the bathhouse we are each given a wire basket to stuff our clothes in after we change. My uncles quickly strip—I don't want to look at them without their pants—and step into their suits. They wear gold crosses around their necks that shimmer in the dense black hair of their chests. Around us, people clamber in and out of clothes. The men's genitals hang from their stomachs like hammers. My uncles ignore me. Surrounded by naked strangers, chlorine, and cigarette smoke, I stand there with my clothes on, holding the basket.

"Get changed," Pat says expressionlessly.

The floor of the bathhouse is a concrete slab. I look down at it.

"You want us to close our eyes?" Lawrence asks.

Pete and Lawrence are smiling when I look up, but not Pat.

"You need help?" he wants to know.

I consider simply running off, but shake my head no and undress, closing my own eyes to avoid the sight of them as I strip, the sight of myself, then fumble into my bathing trunks. My cousins are dressed and already in the pool. Beyond the wooden bathhouse walls, I hear the water and laughter, the intermittent screech of the lifeguards' whistles. We hand our baskets to the attendant and pin a number to our suits so we can later reclaim them, and step through a huge pan of smoky water to delouse our feet.

The pool takes my breath: amethyst, large as a football field, pristine as animation. The ocean I've never seen. I follow my uncles to the deep end where our blankets lie. My mother lies on her stomach, listening to a transistor radio and smoking a cigarette. She leads me down to the shallows and sits dangling her legs into the water while I bob at her feet. Sunlight maps the pool floor with silver shadows. I dive to them and open my eyes, touch the painted blue, and lie there on my belly, happy, untouchable, sealed off in my perfect watery dream. The dead do not accompany us to the pool. They cannot tolerate water. It is a gate, a wall and portal. The dead remain as superstitious as the living, timid as children.

When I come up for breath, my mother is gone. I wander back to the towel, where she sits rubbing Coppertone across her shoulders. My uncles stand in the pool in front of us. They lift my cousins, Pat's two boys and Pete's son, high in the air and fling them into the deep. Each time they're dunked, they swim confidently to the pool's edge, hoist themselves out, and jump back in for more. They stand on their hands, and plunge off the diving board: cannonballs, jackknives, half gainers. From the blanket I watch. Suddenly someone has me—one of my uncles. Lawrence. I know because he is missing the middle finger on his left hand. He picks me up as if I'm no heavier than a two-by-four.

My mother says, "Lawrence," but that's all.

He carries me to the edge. Beneath me are Pat and Pete, standing to their shoulders. Lawrence lifts me above his head. I scream, and he hurls me out into the pool where the bottom is invisible, the water marbled and silent. I know that this is something I'm supposed to accept as if it does not scare me, that boys are meant to be brave, and should never ask for mercy. But I am not brave. I know this from the way my uncles, with their chiseled teeth and black hair, the stubble that blackens their jaws, laugh each time I surface, screaming, trying to get my breath, before they are on me again, their hands like pliers, shaking me above the unrelieved blue expanse. Trapped beneath it, waiting to rise again to air, the water shot through with veins of light and amniotic faces, I realize that they mean to kill me. My mother is on her feet, telling them to stop, but they do not stop until she loses her temper and dives into the pool. Then they relent, standing with just their heads visible as she punches at them and tells them they are sons of bitches. They tell her she should know.

"Fuck you. Especially you," she spits at the white scar on Pat's jaw. He and his brothers laugh and dash water in her face as she lifts me out and carries me, crying, to the blanket.

Many of these things, I don't tell my mother. She would deny them. *Here's what happened*, she would say. Delivering, after all, her birthday present, I don't wish to rob her of the version of truth she clings to. She would defend its existence down to her last breath. It would turn into an argument. I've seen it happen over and over with my parents. A two-hour battle resulting in my mother not speaking to my father, and sometimes me either, over the facts surrounding something that never occurred.

I refrain also from mentioning the dead. She would clap her hands to her ears and tell me to shut my goddam mouth, ask me if I were trying to put the eyes on her. Instead, I tell her how amazing it was to watch her launch herself in a perfect arc off the high dive, and knife through the pool, length upon length, water chipping into the sky above her like bits of broken glass.

"I was a good swimmer," she says. "I was on the swim team at Peabody. Your father can't swim. He's afraid of water."

I have never seen my father in a swimming pool, nor in a pair of bathing trunks. But he would sit in just his boxers in my kiddie pool with me. With water pistols, we shot bees feeding off the clover surrounding the pool. He dropped dimes on its blue floor. Wearing a skin-diver's mask, I'd hold my breath and scour my face across the bottom, searching for the silver while he sat in the water reading the paper, drinking coffee.

My father has always been forthright about himself. "I never learned to swim, Fritzy. Water scares me. It's beautiful, but too much when it's all around me." How odd, I'd think: hearing an adult, my father, confess fear, something my mother would never admit to. When I went to work for Pat, my father told me I was making a mistake. He's afraid of his own shadow, my mother says of my father. Can't change a lightbulb or hang curtain rods. The year after my uncles tried to drown me, my father walked me to Kingsley House down on Auburn Street every morning, where he took swimming lessons in their basement pool. I took an art class while he swam, and made a red and yellow tile mosaic ashtray for my mother's birthday. We didn't attend the family picnic that year, nor ever again.

My mother props her head in the hand that holds her lit cigarette, just above her right eye. She stares expectantly at a spot above my head, and well beyond. A bar of light bisects her face diagonally; smoke snakes around it. She is perfectly still. In a trance. Injected with Sodium Pentothal. Mesmerized. Powerless to lie. Slowly I reach for another Chesterfield. Now is my chance to pry the slab off the crypt of secrets. Now, while this smoke and light bewitch her. What happened, I'll ask her, between you and your mother? How did Fred's shop burn down? What is it between you and Pat? And my father?

But my mother snaps out of it. She is suddenly curious to know what I plan to do with my life now that I've graduated, just a week ago, after an undistinguished four years at Saint Sebastian's, a Catholic high school for boys. I tell her I don't know, which is the unadorned truth. Maybe, she muses, since Pat's boys, in college and already too big for their britches, are showing no interest in his business, maybe Pat will take me under his wing. Who knows, maybe he'll cut me in on the business some day. If I show a little gumption, a little backbone, if I don't mind getting my hands dirty. After the war, Pat started out with nothing, and now he's a millionaire. *Not like your father*, she wants to throw in, but refrains. The day after I graduated, my mother had me call Pat—he didn't even recognize my name—and ask him if he'd hire me to carry a hod. She doesn't even know what a hod is, just that my dad couldn't carry one the year they'd had to get married and Pat put him on the crew. I didn't know what one was either until the first day I stepped up to one and tried to lift it. I don't know. Sometimes I think I'd like to write comic books, like Jack Kirby and Stan Lee, but I can't draw and I never get any further than a few panels of two haggling stick figures: *Travis and Rita.*

RITA: *Let's go to Mass, Travis.*
TRAVIS: *Next Sunday.*
RITA: *No. Today.*
TRAVIS: *It's four o'clock, Rita.*
RITA: *We could find a church that's open. I want Communion.*
TRAVIS: *I don't think we'd be welcome in church, Rita. I think we've had too much of this to drink.*
RITA: *There's such a thing as forgiveness, Travis.*
TRAVIS: *I don't think so.*
RITA: *Why are you being such a smart-shit?*

Or:

TRAVIS: *Pay her no mind, Fritz. All that dago mumbo jumbo.*
RITA: *What is it with you, Travis? All these years and you're still looking down your nose from that mountain of Irish pig shit. I remember your mother: two loaded shopping bags, three buses to get groceries, a secondhand coat, her legs so swollen they looked like pizza dough.*
TRAVIS: *Did I say anything about your mother, Rita?*
RITA: *My mother has always liked you.*
TRAVIS: *I like her too. She knows how to keep her mouth shut.*
RITA: *Not like me.*
TRAVIS: *No, not like you at all. But I'll thank you to not disparage my mother.*
RITA: *Kiss my ass, Travis.*
TRAVIS: *Fine, I'd love to kiss your ass. But enough about my mother.*

I have a lot of them, but they're mere transcription, not art, and, really, who would want to plagiarize the lives of Travis and Rita Sweeney? Still, I can't stop myself.

"Do you remember getting lost?" my mother asks me. "My God, I was out of my mind."

Because of my shame. The bathhouse, my uncles flinging me through the sky into the water, my blubbering in front of Pat's sons. The way my mother stepped out of Pat's Plymouth after changing into her shiny swimsuit with its side zipper open. Enough that Pat saw, and didn't look away. With contempt didn't look away. Like he owns her. Because my father isn't here, but home reading the newspaper, maybe packing his suitcase, not bothering with a note or even the empty formality of farewell, without even the necessary contempt to scrawl *love* or *hate.*

Later, as they all eat and nap and play poker and bocce, I wander away from our pavilion to play in the creek. My grandmother lounges on the bank, her feet washed in its swirl. Despite the heat, she wears a man's gray sweater over one of my grandfather's old white shirts. Gray trousers. She dresses like a man, but she is a woman. Of arresting beauty, yet the years have coated her with an impervious largeness, not the dulled inertia of mere fat, but a grandiosity both patrician and pitiful, that render her iconographic, some unnamed, exiled saint.

Her hair is a scorched flaxen gray, cinched into a bun, no makeup, a stretched severity beneath her eyes, a flawless complexion decidedly the color of creamed coffee. An upper lip that peels off her fine, small teeth in a lovely, sneering smile that would have led men to love her. Much prettier than my mother, she smells of coriander.

She smiles and whispers *Federico* when I plop next to her. With large, flat rocks, smoothed by millennia of slow water, we build a dam across the little creek. We fill an empty pop bottle with creek-sand and water. *Giambotta*, my grandmother calls the concoction, an Italian word that means "big mess," but she is not Italian. She is *Negro, Spanish, Cuban, Syrian, Arab, Indian.* I've heard these words, this speculation, orbit her before, though I cannot pinpoint their origin. My mother denies her mother's darkness. She denies herself. She's Rita Schiaretta, Fred the shoemaker's daughter. Federico, after whom I'm called.

Because I have never had to address her, I have no name for my grandmother. *Ouma,* she insists I call her. There is value in anonymity, she confides. My homeliness is a good thing. She leans over and brushes her lips across my forehead. She asks if I've been baptized. I tell her I don't know. She scoops up a handful of water from the creek and drips it over my head, whispers a melodious, strange-sounding prayer, and declares: "Nothing can harm you now." She kisses me again and pulls me tightly against her warm, ample body.

The dead pace the creek bank. They wear long, heavy overcoats. On their shoulders rests a dusting of snow. Ouma tells me there's nothing to fear, that I should pretend I don't see them. They cross in and out of the world through water. They are kind, but jealous of the living. My grandfather smiles and holds out a hand to me.

"Don't be afraid of him," says Ouma. "Tell him to go away."

He wants me to cross the creek. Behind him mill his cohorts, grizzled in ice. They sit on the swings, climb to the top of the slide and plummet down. Often they cannot hold onto the world, not even for this little bit, and disappear like breath on a windowpane.

"Shoo," Ouma hisses at them. "Shoo away with you."

Finally I take my grandfather's hand and step across the creek to him.

"Federico," Ouma calls, but neither I nor my grandfather turn to acknowledge her summons. That quickly, I am lost, though still I see Ouma peering into the divide, reaching out as if feeling in the dark for a barrier she knows is there.

I play in the sandbox with my grandfather. He removes his coat and loosens his tie. Grave dirt spills from his sleeves. His finely cobbled shoes smolder. I build roads and walls, houses populated with families. Dogs and cars. A church with a cross lording over it, music swelling over its threshold. In the evenings the families I imagine in these houses eat candlelit meals off fine tablecloths. They sleep in bedrooms surrounded by enormous trees that sway all night in the breeze.

My grandfather digs furiously. Sweat boils out of his face and lands sizzling at his feet. He is trying to find something. He is trying to say something. *Rimpianto.* Regret. But he cannot say words. Not in any language. His dead *paisans* beckon, and finally he rises. Sand rains down from him. He dons his coat, raises a hand, and dodders off. I follow as best as I can, but the dead are flimsy. Bits of them blow off in the wind, the sun evaporates them, trees subsume them, they melt. My legs are short. The dead leave no footprints. The sky clogs with clouds like furnaces.

I see my Ouma, there on the other side, tearing at her yellow-gray hair. Undone, it falls about her shoulders, cascades down her back. Her mouth is saying *Federico.* She wrings her hands. I turn and follow the dead, the scraps of smoke they leave behind, the tiny mounds of dust. Through my catechism I have learned that Jesus lives among dead; He sees both worlds. I see both worlds too: the one of *here,* my mother and father's world, Pat's world; and the one of smoke and dirt, the realm of my grandfather, of Jesus, the wordless longing: *rimpianto.* I'm at the edge of the lake, then up to my knees in the water, the clouds now black and bunched. Night-tide in broad daylight. I will swim across this lake to Jesus.

But Jesus cannot outscream my mother, and it is her voice that brings me back into the world of *here.* Her voice not calling my name, but Pat's: *Patrick.* Then mine: *Fritzy* at the top of her voice. Like she's searching for us both, but she's chasing Pat who is headed toward the water, but he doesn't see me. *Patrick,* she calls again, and he stops. She runs full force into him and they both disappear in the water. They are trying to kill each other, their hands searching for each other's throats. They come up and go under. My mother's bathing suit peels down to her waist. Then they are not trying to kill each other. Pat handles her roughly, and she allows it.

"I can't find him," she screams, then punches at his face.

"We'll find him," Pat says. "He's okay." He holds my mother's wrists. Her breasts are bare, white as paper plates against her dark arms and shoulders. Her vaccination scar looks like the Miraculous Medal.

Then they spy Ouma, still digging at her head, at the lip of the lake, staring at its implacable green. Pat lets go of my mother's arms. She pulls her bathing suit up; the straps still hang. Ouma turns toward them and simply points toward the lake.

"Mom," I yell, but perhaps the wind now roiling up takes my cry, because no one hears.

"Where's Fritzy, Mama?" asks my mother. "I can't find him."

"In between," says Ouma.

"You crazy witch," my mother fires, and races into the water. She thrashes along its surface. She dives again and again. Each time she comes up, screaming my name. I call, but she doesn't hear. The storm bulls in at twenty knots, the lake whitecapping, Ouma's hair and big clothes flapping off her.

Rain pummels the earth; it claws off the lake like shrapnel. My mother is a foot from me. I can see her as through a sliding glass door, the shutter of an immense camera. *Fritzy,* she screams over and over, Pat trying to keep her away, lightning lighting their faces like doppelgangers, like the crossed-over. And then my mother reaches in, clasps my hand, and I step out of the lake and into her arms.

"I found you," my mother says.

I take another Chesterfield, and light it off hers. She smiles at me, as if proud of my knack with cigarettes. Even with the birds, we can hear my father snoring. A thunderous, phlegmy rip every two seconds.

"Jesus Christ," she mumbles, then: "You hear him? Sometimes I want to kill him. Just take something and shut his wind off."

I've heard these kinds of cracks out of her all my life: how she'd like to kill my dad. But she says it about herself too, and with more relish. She'll shoot herself or jump off a bridge. She'll interrupt one of the few meals we ever have together to announce that she'd like to stick a knife in her chest, then with a look of vindication mime the action: the imaginary blade in her hand as she digs out her heart.

"I found you," she says again.

I don't feel found at all. I'm waiting for the sound of Shotty's horn and another interminable day wobbling under the hot sun, the weight of the hod driving me down while Pat watches silently, unmoved as brick. Sitting at the kitchen table with my mother, I feel like any minute I might stumble into that realm of the dead again.

My mother carries me to the pavilion. She holds me while they sing "Happy Birthday" above the storm. There must have been cake, but I don't remember the cake. I don't remember candles, nor my mother blowing them out, nor wishes. My mother is not the type to make a wish. She lives in the *here,* where suffering is guaranteed. I am curled against her wet bathing suit, the clammy warmth of her neck. She closes her eyes and sings along with everyone else. I look out at my family, but they are merely the dead. Strangers. And then I shut my eyes. Some day I'll find out that today, Decoration Day, is not, in fact, my mother's birthday, that her name is not Rita at all.

There are times when I look in the mirror and wonder if Pat is my father. But Pat has rakish good looks; my face is plain, forgettable. I have the flat nose and high cheeks of my father. His Irish blue eyes. I'm Travis Sweeney's son. Trying to establish my own *here,* I say this to myself. I say *Travis. Rita.* I say my own name. As if the sound of these names tethers me to existence. There are hardly any baby pictures. No pictures really. No wedding. No honeymoon. There is no way to establish what happened. Just words, and then finally silence.

For an instant the light fades from the kitchen; the birds stop singing. I'm sure I hear thunder, but it is the vibrato of my father's massive snores. Still, it could rain. The sky could let loose with enough dark and clamor and water to wash this entire day away. I would not have to leave for the construction site. I would stay home with my mother and father, who have the holiday off.

We would celebrate my mother's birthday. I would go out under an umbrella and buy her a decent robe.

Soon my father will appear in the doorway, rubbing a hand across his face. He'll say, "Happy birthday, Rita," and offer to bake a cake. He'll rummage through the cabinets.

"What are you doing?" my mother will demand.

"Baking your birthday cake."

"Like hell. You didn't remember."

"I beg your pardon, Rita. If I hadn't remembered, I wouldn't have gotten out of bed earlier than usual to bake you a cake. Would I?"

"That's a goddam cover-up for the fact that you forgot. Admit it, gutless wonder."

"Your logic is breathtaking, Rita. You're mysterious as Confucius."

"Kiss my ass, Travis."

"Happy birthday, Rita."

Another *Travis and Rita.*

Then the birds are back, and the light, razoring through the curtains, torching my mother's face and hair. She shields her eyes. It's another working day. This entire time I've been doodling on a napkin, drawing a hod. I draw it the way my father taught me to draw a house: a rectangle with a V-thatch roof atop it. Then I turn the drawing over: a hod is like a house upside down, all the food and furniture and people emptied out, and in their places brick and mortar. I pencil in the pole you clutch to shoulder the hod. Shotty leans on the horn of his Bonneville. I get to my feet and place the napkin in front of my mother.

"This is what a hod looks like," I tell her.

"I don't believe you," she answers, stirring that knife around in her chest.

I want to say, *I love you, Mother.* I want to guide her hand up to my face and hold it there. Instead, I say, "Happy birthday, Mom," give her a kiss, and head for the door.

ATAVIA

I stand in the middle of our shrunken yard holding the hose nozzle, geared to spray, straight up at the sky. The water falls back down over me in a gentle rain silvered by the late afternoon sun that hunkers in the firmament like the flaming entry to the other side. A few feet away, my parents sit on stained green and white striped lawn chairs. As I peer through the sleeve of mist enveloping me, they lapse in and out of focus. On the tiny rusted table between them are a radio, cigarettes, and a bottle of liqueur called *atavia.* It is the color of Merthiolate and possesses the same terrifying smell.

My mother wants a baby, but she cannot conceive because someone has put the eyes on her. She consulted with Graziella, the neighborhood *strega.* Graziella makes the *atavia,* which means, according to my mother, "to your life." She handed my mother the bottle with the instructions that she and her *amatore,* my father, each drink one cordial glass of it before retiring, every night until the bottle is spent. Graziella was explicit and grave, wagging a long flimsy finger in my mother's face. "And, do not forget. Pray to God and trust to nature. *Appassionato.*"

But my parents don't drink with that kind of restraint. They quickly forget about Graziella's formula for the *bambino.* They'll drain the entire bottle this burning afternoon, and then there will be too much *amore.* My mother tilts her head and closes her eyes. Mascara mats like dust in her lashes. She wears a black bathing suit top, a flimsier version of her black brassieres, and a pair of too-tight red shorts that crimp her rubbery midriff. Violet veins scrag up and down her thick legs. Lacquered red toenails.

My father, bare-chested, his belly crayon-white, his shoulders hot pink from the sun, wears bedroom slippers and khakis. On his left arm is a tattooed heart. *Rita,* my mother's name, rips through it, then an arrow. He holds both her hands as they kiss. When they come away from each other, she seems almost shy, self-conscious. She looks at me and smiles, but I make no sign that I've noticed. They drink from shot glasses stenciled with monkeys hanging by their tails from a tree branch, *Bottoms Up* scrawled beneath the monkeys.

The radio is tuned to WAMO, Pittsburgh's black station. Porky Chedwick, the WAMO DJ, "your platter-pushin' papa," announces that it's 98 degrees. All afternoon, he's spun 45s like "Heat Wave," "Summer in the City," "Hot Fun in the Summertime." Between songs, Porky plays the WAMO jingle: *Whatta you know? You know W-A-M-O.* My mother points toward a lone patch of fleecy clouds and says, "Those clouds look like a man and woman about to explode."

When "The Long Hot Summer" pours out of the radio, they rise and dance. My mother rests her head on my father's shoulder, wraps both hands around his neck. Her mouth moves to the song. His chin rests on her head, an inch of cigarette smoldering between his lips. Eyes closed, he sweats heavily. They drag across the parched yard. The grass, what's left of it, has gone to clover, long stocks topped with brown, shriveled buds swarming with bees.

Bees light on my mother's bare feet, my father's slippers. Bees along the rims of their shot glasses, along the bottle neck as well. Bees climb their legs and roost in their hair. They sit on my father's closed eyelids, on my mother's lips as she soundlessly sings. I can see that Graziella's potion has taken hold. There's sure to be a baby now.

ACKNOWLEDGMENTS

Grateful acknowledgment is extended to the following journals, in which some of these stories, or earlier versions of them, first appeared:

Beloit Fiction Journal: "Thy Womb Jesus"
The Chattahoochee Review: "Lover"
Davidson Miscellany: "The School for the Blind"
Italian Americana: "Zeppole"
The Pittsburgh Quarterly: "Killers"
The Rambler: "Decoration Day"
River Walk Journal: "Scaffold"
The Southeast Review: "Atavia"
The Sun: "Fading Away," "The High Heart," and "Hod"
West Branch: "Epiphany"

Lines from these stories, often in appreciably different form, appeared in poems published in *West Branch* and in the author's *This Metal* (Laurinburg, NC: St. Andrews College Press, 1996).

Photograph: Jan Hensley

ABOUT THE AUTHOR

Born and raised in Pittsburgh, Joseph Bathanti came to North Carolina in 1976 as a VISTA volunteer to work in the state's prison system and later earned an MFA in creative writing from Warren Wilson College, in Swannanoa. He is the author, most recently, of two novels—*Coventry*, for which he received the 2006 Novello Literary Award, and *East Liberty*, which won the 2001 Carolina Novel Award—and a work of nonfiction, *They Changed the State: The Legacy of North Carolina's Visiting Artists, 1971–1995*, published in 2007 by the North Carolina Arts Council. He has also written four volumes of poetry, among them *This Metal*, which was nominated for a National Book Award, as well as the one-act play *Afomo*, which won the Wachovia Playwrights Prize and was produced by the Lab Theatre of the University of Tennessee at Knoxville. The recipient of numerous other honors, among them the Samuel Talmadge Ragan Award, presented annually for outstanding sustained contributions to the fine arts of North Carolina, the Linda Flowers Prize, the Sara Henderson Hay Prize, and the Sherwood Anderson Award, he teaches creative writing at Appalachian State University, in Boone, North Carolina.